This story though fiction is ded
great grandmother Nancy Christman weliever who in 1804
arrived in the little town of Darlington Indiana along with
her younger brother Billy. She and her family had driven a
covered wagon from Pennsylvania and had stopped for a
short time on the banks of Sugar Creed. Mr. Weliever had
wanted to continue west but Mrs. Weliever had said she
would go no further so they settled there and built a small
home.

Grams was a true pioneer in every sense of the word,
always wearing a broach at the throat and high lace up
ladies shoes. I remember her making her own soap and
candles and reading her Bible by lamplight while setting in
her rocker.

It was and is women like her who are the strength of this
great country and will be so until freedom is nothing more
than a memory.

Copper Penny

In July of 1883 the west was still wild and the state of Indiana was baking as usual. The corn was knee high as it should be, and the town of Crawfordsville was about its normal business. The old steamers whistle blew as engine fifty seven slowed, belched black coal smoke and released her steam before she finally stopped in front of the Monon Station platform on Market Street. The porter rolled the big steel wheeled cart across the platform toward the baggage car and stood waiting patiently for the door to open so he could begin unloading.

The copper skin, shoulder length black hair and hard

muscular line of his jaw did nothing to detract from the smile on the face of the man looking out the passenger car window at the incredibly beautiful woman now standing on the platform. The woman trying to see through the steam was his mother, and she was still as beautiful as ever. Her hands clasp in front of her one moment and waving frantically the next made Richard Running Elk Weliever Stratton realize he had indeed been gone longer than he should have. It had been almost a year since Elk's last visit and he hadn't written as often as he should have, but he knew she would say nothing about that. What she would do is ask about his father, and his people. She would call him Richard instead of Elk or R.E. as U.S. Marshal Jack Cunningham did. Cook for him and do his laundry, but mostly, she would ask about the west.

Nancy Weliever had a good life in Indiana, but at heart she was still that young pioneer woman who had driven that wagon west with her son Pete. She would be that woman until her las.t day. Women like her had built this country, and would continue to be its strength until freedom was just a memory.

"Richard"! She yelled, as the handsome young man stepped off the train onto the platform.

He picked her up in his strong arms and whirled her around. "Hello mother. I've missed you".

"Put me down Richard, people are looking".

"Let them. They will see the most beautiful woman in this whole territory. Being hugged by a big Indian. Give em' something to talk about at suppertime. Bet most of these folks never even seen an Indian before".

"They have so. You were raised here or have you forgotten that young man"?

"Elk laughed. How could I? Running around in war paint terrorizing the neighbors. Lucky I didn't have us all thrown in jail. How's pop"?

Upon Nancy's return from Oregon, she had met and married a man named Oliver Stratton. He had accepted not only a single woman with an Indian boy, but had taken both into his heart. He had treated Elk as if he was his own son and the youngster had responded in kind.

"He's fine, asked about you all the time. He is gone a lot lately. They have built a new line up north and he has been traveling back and forth checking on the tracks and hiring men for the day run between here and somewhere north of Chicago. I'll be glad when he's through with it. I don't like being home alone all the time; you're going to stay for a while aren't you Richard. I know Oliver will want to see you"?

The truth is mother, Marshal Cunningham sent for me. Seems he has some work for me. Say's its important. I'm headed that way in the morning".

Elk pulled a leather bag from under his coat and handed it to his mother. "Running Elk sends his best. Says he hopes to see you one of these days".

Nancy took the bag of gold and placed it in her purse. "Do you have any idea how much gold your father has sent me over the last twenty years? I have gotten a bag just like this every year. People at the bank get nervous when they see me coming. Gold isn't something you see here in this town, and there are more than a few who would like to know where it comes from".

Elk's face took on a serious look. "They been asking questions mother"?

"Not of me, but Oliver has been questioned some. Nothing direct, they aren't that forward, but this gold is refined, and they have been very curious. Oliver thought he had seen someone watching him, and following him around the last time he went north. I don't see how that could be though.

We haven't said anything about this to anyone. A person has to use these banks. I couldn't just dig a hole in the yard and bury it".

Elk turned and looked at his mother. "Mom, you head on home. I have a short errand and then I'll be along. I have to pick up a horse at the livery anyway".

Nancy smiled. "Bill will be glad to see you. He hasn't changed a bit. A little grumpy these days but that's about it. I think he and Zac are going to live forever".

The young man kissed her on the cheek and headed up Market Street toward the livery. As he approached, he could see Bill Allison setting out in front with his chair tilted back against the wall. Elk eased himself up along the side of the building and peeked around the corner.

"If you're thinkin' of sneakin' up on me young man, you're gonna' have to come in from the other direction. Besides I seen your mother headed for the station. She told me you was comin' in today".

Elk stepped around the corner and shook the old man's hand.

"I declare son, you look just like your father. Might taller, but got that same look and walk about you. How is the Chief anyway? And what you doin' back here? Thought you was out there for good".

"He is fine Bill. And I'm here on business. You heard from Zac"?

"Yep. Well not from him exactly. Pete writes now and again. He's the same as me I reckon. Old".

"You two will never change Bill. You have any good stock I can buy? Something that will last. I might be in the saddle for quite a spell, and I need a good horse".

The old man smiled. "Got just the thing son. Thought about keepin' this one for myself, but don't spend that much time in the saddle no more. Not that I couldn't mind you. Just don't want to".

Elk grinned as the old timer disappeared into the shop. He returned leading a tall well muscled animal. "Son, this here is what they call a Tennessee walker. Some name ain't it. Fact is, this horse has a way of steppin' out and coverin' a lot of territory without warin' himself out. Good gate, and easy on the seat of your pants".

Elk looked the animal over. "He is beautiful Bill. How do you think he will do on the long haul? If I have to head across country"?

The old man rubbed his chin and thought for a minute, then looked up. "I got it son. It ain't here right now, and I'll have to go to Darlington to get it. One of the Patton boys has a pony that was shipped in from Louisiana with his cows. Don't know why it come, but it did. Looks to me like the old pony's we used to ride out west. Little wild, but nothin' you can't handle. Have it here tomorrow".

Elk shook the old timers hand and headed for town. When he got to Washington Street he turned left and headed for the bank. The barbershop in the hotel was full, and every head turned as this tall well dressed Indian walked past the window.

The face in the dark suit setting behind the desk at the bank wasn't familiar to him. As Elk walked through the door into the man's office, he smelled cigar smoke.

The man got up and came around the desk with his hand outstretched. Making a show of being friendly. He covered the distance between them with hand outstretched. The handshake was about what Elk expected. Wet and weak. A sure sign of what was to come.

"Rolland Thomas, at your service sir. Please come in. What can we do for you"?

Elk noticed the chair on this side of the desk was wooden with no arms, and the one behind the desk was large and made from the finest leather. He pulled the chair around to the side of the desk and sat facing the man.

"Mr. Thomas. My name is Richard Running Elk Weliever Stratton. You ever hear of me"?

The man hadn't said anything yet and there was already sweat above his upper lip. Elk noticed this and decided to have his say.

"You folks been watching my mother, and asking questions of my father about their gold. I want to know why you are doing that".

The man's hands were visibly shaking, but he managed to keep his voice steady. "I don't know what you mean by that. Your parents have been banking here even before I bought this bank. They are valued customers and I resent your accusations".

There was no eye contact, but it was a good speech. Elk decided to press a little.

"Let's cut through the crap here Thomas. As you can see, I'm Indian. I was raised here by my mother, but I'm Indian. If you or whoever it is you represent, bother my mother. I will hang you by your feet in a tree and skin you like the rabbit you are". He got up started to walk out of the office, but stopped when the man spoke.

"I know exactly who you are young man. The little boy conceived in the wilderness by your mother and a filthy savage. Bet your mother had a time explaining that to Oliver Stratton. You're the bastard from Wyoming".

Elk looked at the man and smiled. "Well, there it is". Once again prejudice had reared its ugly head. Elk and his mother had been dealing with this for years, from people who didn't know them or the circumstances, or reason for his birth.

The bank guard Ed Smith could see his boss stretched out on top of his desk through the open door to his office. He hadn't seen Elk since he had left for college in New York somewhere. The tall Indian spotted him as he was coming across the lobby, and waved hello.

"Hi Elk. Here to visit your Mother again".

"Hi Ed. Yes, actually I have some business up state. How are your folks"?

"Fine. What's the matter with Thomas there"?

"He's resting. We had a talk and he got tired. "

"Uh huh. You know Elk, I've seen folks do that from time to time through the years when they've been talkin' to you. You must really be a bore".

The two men laughed and Elk walked out of the bank and headed for his mother's place on West Market.

The evening was spent in conversation about Elk's father and the people Nancy knew in the Shoshone Town. Of Elks half brother Pete and the tragedy of his family being murdered. Pete was still somewhere in the southwest hunting down the killers. It had been four years since that incident. He and Zac had stopped at the village while headed south to pick up what supplies they needed since their place had been burned.

The lamps had burned long into the night before Elk said goodnight to his mother and turned in.

Nancy rose early in the morning expecting to fix one of her famous breakfasts only to find the young man gone and a note explaining he would return when he could.

Nancy read the note and smiled. Her mind going back to that impulsive young woman who didn't let any grass grow under her feet either, when there was a job to be done. Sighing, she thought. "I'll see him when I see him".

Elk was standing outside of the livery when Bill came in from the Darlington road leading the horse he went after.

"Bill, that pony looks like he came right out of the mountains. How in the devil do you reckon he got clear back here"?

"Who knows? Strong ain't he? Look at them eyes son. This horse ain't been rode in a while, if ever. Might be he was just plain to ornery to break. This could be real interesting'. I'll put a saddle on him and you can give him a go," The horse was about average size and to Elk looked to have come right off the range. He could tell the animal had been ridden before, but it had been some time by the looks of it. When the animal bunched his back, it was very evident he didn't want any part of this young man.

"Bill, this horse has come out of the mountains somewhere. Look at the muscles in his front and hindquarters. Don't get that from flatland horses. Had to do some climbing to get that well developed. When I get in the saddle, how about you opening the gate. I'm going to start him out the Waynetown road".

Bill walked over and got ready to open the gate. Elk climbed on and the horse bunched once more, gave about three lunges and headed for the gate.

It took a couple of miles for the animal to settle down and get used to the way Elk rode. The way it responded, he was almost sure this animal had been ridden by one of the people. No ordinary horse would have known the knee signals he was getting, or allow its rider to ride, hanging in one stirrup and firing across its chest the way he was now doing. He pulled up and patted the animal's neck. "Reckon them Patton boys didn't know what he had in you son. We're going to ride a ways together. Get you a new pair of shoes and we'll be ready to go".

That afternoon after Elk had taken his mother to the restaurant at the Monon Hotel, he headed for Lafayette to see U.S. Marshal Jack Cunningham.

Jack Cunningham was a big man with broad shoulders and an infectious smile. He had a way about him that set folks at ease and qualified him more for a politician than captain of the U.S. Marshals in this area. He was getting a little long in the tooth now, but there had been a time when to draw down on him was certain to get you planted in the local grave yard. Strapped to his hip was a heavy framed Dragoon. As fast with his gun as he was with his smile, had earned him a reputation as a hard man to deal with. Especially, if you were on the wrong side of the law.

He looked up from a late supper in time to see the deputy tie his horse off in front of the hotel and walk inside.

The marshal sent the waiter over to the hotel after Elk and waited for him to come across the street to join him.

"Evenin' R.E., long trip"?

Elk reached across the table shook hands and pulled up a chair. "Yes it was. Stopped off for a couple of days to see my mother. She sends her love".

The marshal shook his head and grinned. "There ain't but one Nancy Weliever in this whole world. Oliver sure did get lucky when he landed that one. I remember when she took them mules and that dog and run them people up north during the war? With them folks from Georgia chasin' her. Lord what grit".

"I don't mean to cut you short Jack, but you called me away from the most beautiful place on earth. I know it must be important".

The marshal held up his hand. "Not here son. Even these walls have ears these days. Let's go over to the office. This concerns your father, and I don't mean Oliver. I can tell by the expression on your face, this is going to be a long night. C'mon' son".

When the marshal walked through the door to his office, he asked the deputy to see that no one disturbed them. "I'd be obliged Tom, if you'd round up Doc Humphrey for me. See if you can keep folks out of here for a while so me and R.E.

here can have us a talk".

The young man picked up his chair and went out, closing the door behind him.

"Good man Tom. He'll have my job someday".

"Have a seat R.E., we need to talk, and I ain't real sure how to get it started".

The marshal poured himself a small shot of whiskey and downed it before he went on.

"R.E., I got me a bad situation here. About two months ago some folks from over around Battle Ground come in here carrying an old man in the back of their wagon. He was almost gone then, but before he died, he told Doc Humphrey something I been tryin' to keep quiet ever since. The doc will tell you about it, but the short of it is, that old man was killed for a map he was carrying. A map showing the location of a mighty big stash of gold. The location is somewhere near your people in Wyoming territory.

Surprised showed on the young marshals face. "That's supposed to be Spanish gold Jack, and it's been there for three hundred years, maybe longer than that. How could anybody know about it"?

The marshal held up his hand. "I know son. I'm gettin' to that part. Seems this old man had been a sailor or something. Sailed around the world and all that. Least way that's what he told them folks that was haulin' him to the Doc's. Anyway he ran across this map while he was in Spain or somewhere, and decided to see if there was anything to it. He was on his way west when he ran a foul of those that done him in and stole the map".

"That sure sounds farfetched to me Jack. You have got to have more than that to send for me. What's this about my father Running Elk being in trouble? I don't understand that part at all".

"It seemed strange to me too, R.E. until I remembered you

tellin' me about your mother getting those leather sacks of gold all these years. They had to come from somewhere, and I figured there might just be something to this map business.

I don't want to upset you none, but I've had a man watching your mother, and Oliver, for the past few weeks. Seems Oliver has been questioned a time or two about the gold. Matter of fact he came in here and talked to me about it not more than two hours ago. Got him over at the hotel now waiting for you to come in so we can have a talk".

The door swung open and Doc Humphrey came into the office. Elk shook hands and told him he would get back to him later. He walked out with the marshal following him and headed for the hotel.

If what the marshal had told him was true, both Oliver and his mother were in danger. If that was the case, he was going to have to move fast.

Two

Oliver Stratton's room overlooked the street, and just now he was watching his stepson and the marshal walk across the street toward the hotel. He reached over and poured himself a drink, downed it, and waited for the two men to knock on his door.

When Elk entered the room, the man was visibly moved to see him. "I'm glad you're here son. I'm sorry about this trouble. I asked the marshal to send for you. As close as this thing is to your mother, I thought you should get involved. Seems to go all the way to your people. I don't know what can be done, but I'm worried about your mother".

Elk walked over and gave the man a hug. "Glad to see you dad. We'll work through this together. Don't worry. I'm not going to let anything happen to you or mother. Tell me what's been happening".

Oliver walked over and sat back down in the chair staring out the window. Gathering his courage, he turned and faced his stepson.

"It all started about four or five months ago. Rolland Thomas bought the bank in town and right away he became curious about the gold your mother keeps in her safety deposit box. You know how she is Elk. If she needs something, or wants to help someone out, she goes to the bank and gets out a little gold and pays in dust. It's no secret she gets gold every year from your father. Even the post office knows about when it will come. After all, it's been going on for over twenty years. My God son, she has more gold in that bank than anybody in the territory. Elk, your mother has more money in that bank than the banker himself. Anyway about three months ago I was on a track inspection, usually I sleep in one of the cars, but this time there was a section that wasn't complete. In order for me to make my report I had to stay out there over night. About three in the morning I woke up to a light shining in my face and men asking questions about your mother's gold.

"What kind of questions"?

"Where it comes from. Was it processed? Had it been fired? That kind of thing. They roughed me up pretty good and in the end I'm afraid I answered their questions".

Stratton's words trailed off in shame and he bowed his head into his hands.

Elk walked over and put his hand on his shoulder and squeezed. "Dad, if you hadn't answered their questions, they would have beaten the answers out of you anyway. The thing I don't understand is why mother's money interest them".

Jack Cunningham was leaned back against the dresser in the rooms only other chair. When he leaned forward the legs slammed the wooden floor with a thud. "That ain't it R.E. These men don't give two hoots what your mother has in the bank. They were finding out where the gold came from and whether or not it was refined. When they found out, it had been fired. They knew they were on the right track.

My guess is that whole bunch is headed toward that town you folks live in, right now. If that's the case, we need to get a telegram off pronto. The marshal there can alert Running Elk and you can begin trackin' em'".

Elk nodded his agreement. "Might be right at that Jack. I'll get some sleep and head out the first thing in the morning. Dad, you try to get some sleep too, and tomorrow it might be a good idea if you start home. It's not a good idea to leave mother alone with all this going on".

Stratton nodded his head and sighed. "I only wish I had been stronger for her son. If anything happens, it will be my fault".

"Nothin' is going to happen. Jack here has someone watching mother. If anything starts, the deputy will get into the middle of it" Stratton's head came up and he smiled. "I might have known you would be on top of this marshal. Thanks".

"Not a problem Oliver, get some rest".

The two men left and headed for the livery to put Elk's horse up for the night. Cunningham looked to be in deep thought. "What's on your mind Jack"?

"R.E., I'll tell you the truth. If that wasn't your mother's husband in there. Well, let's just say that's the only reason I believe him,"

"Uh huh, it was burnin' me too. Not a pretty thought is it"?

"Thing is Elk, if it's true, what's he after"?

"Jack, the old stories tell of Spanish gold. Not just some, but tons of it. So much that even the Indians don't tell others because they know what will happen. So just the chief and maybe one other person know where it's hidden. That way the secret stays safe".

"And your father knows where it's hidden"?

"Uh huh".

"And who's the other person? Medicine man"?

"No Jack. It's me".

"You reckon Oliver knows that"?

"He couldn't know it. Nobody knows it. Except you now".

"Where do you start R.E"?

"I don't exactly know. I got a couple of things to do Jack. I'll see you in the morning".

"Good night R.E".

"Night Jack".

Elk checked his pony at the livery and went to the hotel, checked into a room and went to bed.

He heard the footsteps approaching his door before he

heard the knock. When he opened it there was a Colt forty five in his fist.

"What's the trouble Jack"?

"Get your clothes on son. Your mother is gone and Rolland Thomas has been shot. He's hanging on but not by much".

Elk dressed and ran downstairs to find the marshal waiting in the lobby with Oliver Stratton.

Jack nodded. "Figure we better take Oliver with us. You go on ahead son. I got a team and buggy outside. Be right on your tail".

Elk ran outside, leaped in the saddle of his already waiting horse and started south to cover the thirty or so miles between Lafayette and Crawfordsville. He had to question Rolland Thomas before it was too late. Somehow he was tied into this, and Elk needed to have that information.

It was just after daylight when the Indian pony crossed Sugar Creek and started up the hill toward his mother's house at three hundred and a half West Market.

The door was open and Nancy's torn apron was on the kitchen floor, along with her ten gauge scattergun.

In spite of the trouble, Elk smiled to himself. He knew that if Nancy had reached the weapon sooner, the problem would have already been solved. His mind flashed back for a moment to his childhood. It had been his mother who had taught him about firearms.

He snapped out of it and headed for the doctor's office. He burst through the door only to find Thomas gone. The doc was there and held up his hand.

"Too late son. Died about an hour ago. He had been hit badly. Could do nothing but make him comfortable".

The disappointment was plain on Elk's face. "Did he say anything Doc"?

"Couldn't shut him up. Matter of fact if I could have, he might still be here. Never seen anybody so mad about dying".

Elk waited for the man to continue.

"Said he was supposed to get part of the gold and was double crossed. Mentioned Oliver and your mother too. Said Oliver was a fool. If it weren't for him, none of this would have happened. What do you think he meant by that son"?

Elk didn't answer and turned to leave.

"Son, Thomas said something else".

Elk waited.

"Said if they didn't get the gold, they would kill your mother. The last thing out of his mouth was Indianapolis".

That last statement told Elk all he needed to know. When he stepped out on the porch, Cunningham was just pulling up in the buckboard.

Elk walked over, grabbed Oliver's coat front and jerked him out. "I want the story Oliver, and I want it now".

The man's face contorted in fear and had lost all color.

"Son, I should have told you sooner but I was afraid. They threatened to kill me and your mother".

"Yeah, well now they have her. Talk Oliver, I'm out of patience".

"On the trips I take up north. Well, this bunch was friendly to me and I started playing cards. Before I knew it I was in over my head and they threatened me. I told your mother and she gave me some of the gold to pay the debt, but I had to promise her I would never gamble again. My mistake was, I paid them in gold. They took one look at it and wanted to know where I got it. When I wouldn't tell them, they beat me until I did. They got next to Thomas somehow and the next thing I know here you are, and Nancy's gone. It got out of hand Elk, and it was my fault. God, what have I done"?

The man broke down and collapsed against the wagon in

tears.

Despite his anger, Elk loved this man who had taken his mother and him in so long ago. He put his arm around his shoulder.

"Dad, what you did was stupid, but very human. These people just saw you coming is all. I'm not happy about what has happened, but what we have to do now is get mother back. It may be dangerous, but whatever it takes, we have to do".

"Whatever you want son. I do love her so".

Elk turned to Cunningham. "Jack, Thomas said Indianapolis. I figure they are holed up somewhere in the city. We are going to need some help".

Cunningham turned and headed up the street. "Leave that to me son. You roust Bill out and get some fresh mounts. Be back in a minute".

Three

Oliver's house on Market Street smelled of fresh baked bread. Nancy had turned in at her regular time, but couldn't sleep. There had been just too much excitement with Elk coming home. Oliver should be in on the morning train, and she was looking forward to the reunion among the three of them.

She reached over and turned up the lamp, got out of bed, dressed and went to the kitchen. Put some wood in the stove and adjusted the draft.

The cupboard where she kept her cooking supplies had just been filled and she pulled down the cinnamon, sugar, crushed walnuts, and some raisins.

*The bread dough was kept ready in a large crock by the sink, and covered with a wet cloth to keep it fresh. She set the dough on the breadboard and worked it out. Sprinkled in a handful of sugar mixed with cinnamon and flower, then threw in some walnuts and raisins and began to form the loaves.

She had just pulled the three golden brown loaves out of the oven and was brushing butter on the top when she heard the knock on the kitchen door. A smile came to her face, she smoothed back her hair and walked over and unlocked the back door.

"Richard, it's about time you got back here". Nancy pulled the door open and found herself staring onto the face of a stranger.

The ten gauge she kept behind the door hadn't been used in a long while, but it was always kept primed and ready. She reached for it, only to be knocked off balance by the door being forced open.

The scattergun fell to the floor and went off, blowing two of the legs off the kitchen table and throwing the freshly baked bread to the floor.

Nancy went for the meat cleaver lying on the counter, but was grabbed by the back of the hair and thrown across the room. She came off the wall with her fist clenched only to be backhanded and thrown to the floor. The pain in her left wrist was caused by the stranger's right foot.

"Lady if you don't want me to break your arm, you lay real still. Smith get that dish rag and tie her mouth shut I've had about all of her I want, at least for now".

The man bent down and smiled at her. His breath smelled like dead animals and his teeth were rotting in his mouth. Nancy spit in the man's face and tried to kick him in the groin. He grabbed her hair and pulled her up just far enough to hit her in the face. She heard ringing in her ears and everything began to dim, and finally go black.

A groan escaped her lips as she was roughly thrown over his shoulder. "Smith, grab them loaves of bread. No use in lettin' em' go to waste".

"Right Max. She is a hellcat ain't she? Little gray, but might be more there than we can see right now". The two men laughed and threw her into the back of the wagon.

"That shot is goin' to bring the law. Better hightail it for Indianapolis. Head north there toward Garfield and then we'll cut back over and catch the Mace road. And don't be goin' too fast. I don't want no trouble. We get caught with a tied up woman in this wagon, and we'll swing from the nearest tree. Won't have to worry none about a trial. Get movin'".

"What about the banker"?

"Moor and Stony got that end of it. He's dead by now. Besides folks will be over lookin' at him. By the time the law gets here we'll be long gone. I ain't goin' to tell you again Smith, get this wagon movin'. And hand me one of them loaves".

Nancy came back around sometime before dawn and lay quiet in the wagon, listening to the men talk and trying as best she could to recognize what little she saw of the countryside.

She couldn't believe how stupid these two were. They had not even taken the time to throw a tarp over her. Her face was swollen and her right shoulder had been rubbed raw from being bounced around in the wagon. It was sometime after noon before the wagon stopped. She felt someone grab her ankles and begin pulling her out of the wagon. The fall to the ground knocked the wind out of her and it took a minute to get it back.

Rotten mouth walked over and looked down at her. "Ain't so tough now, are you old woman. I think I'm just goin' to take you right here". He placed one foot on either side of her and reached for his belt buckle.

This time her aim was true. Her right foot came up with all the power she could muster and caught him between the legs. Nancy heard the breath catch in his throat and smiled a little, when he keeled side wammnf4ys and hit the ground, holding himself and vomiting.

Hearing laughter, she turned her head in an effort to see who it was. The sun was shining in her eyes and all she could see was the darkened figure above her.

"Mrs. Stratton, I am Mr. McFarland. You and I are going to do some business together. I see by the way you just handled Max there. The two of them were lucky to even get you here. We'll make you comfortable inside where it's a bit cooler".

The man nodded to Smith and she was jerked roughly to her feet and led inside. There was nothing in the barn but a table, part of an old wagon and some chairs. Nancy was tied to one and set back out of the way.

McFarland came back around and this time she had a look

at him. True to his name, he had red hair and green eyes. Dressed in a brown expensive looking suit complete with ivory handled cane. He had an arrogant way about him Nancy had seen before. This was the kind of man who was for no one but himself. She already hated him.

"Mrs. Stratton, you are a wealthy woman. In possession of more than a little gold, and know the location of even more. Your halfbreed son knows we have you and is bringing us what you have in the bank. You're here because you are going to tell me where the rest of it is. After that you will be released and may go on your way. Now, where does the gold come from? And how much is there"?

Nancy looked at McFarland and laughed out loud.

He stepped forward and slapped her hard across the face, knocking her and the chair over backwards. He nodded to Smith and the man set her upright again.

She had run out of patience. "Do you have any idea what you're doing? My son's people will hunt you down and skin you like a possum. You're a fool McFarland. Turn me loose now, while you're still able".

The man laughed, walked over and slapped her again. "I bet you get tired of this before I do Mrs. Stratton. I may just let Max here have a go at you if you don't show a little more respect. What do you think Max"?

Nancy looked over at the filthy man, the sight of him made her ill. She was going to have to find some way to stall these men, and stay alive. Whatever it took. The thought of this filthy man was more than she could bear. She leaned her head forward and closed her eye's. For the first time she could remember, there was no one by her side. Right this minute, she felt very much alone.

*My great grandmother made bread like this when I was a lad. She also made all of her own candles and soap. Her people settled in this part of the country and had many

Indian friends. I am sure many of the meals I had as a boy came from Native American recipes.

Four

The livery at the end of Market Street was dark when Elk got there. As he approached, he noticed the gate to the coral was open, and the stock though not out, could have been. Having been raised around Bill Allison and knew he was not the kind to be that careless.

The forty five was in his hand almost before he went into the crouch and stepped quickly into the shadows. A quick look in the side window gave no clue either. Working his way around to the front he eased the door open just enough to slip inside. It took a moment for the young marshal to adjust his eyes to the darkness, and that was a moment too long. The gun barrel that had just split his skin above the right ear would also send him into darkness, but not before he had heard the name that would give him the only lead he had to go on.

"McFarland said not to kill him, you fool. Now clear these horses out of here and let's get goin'. We got a four hour ride ahead of us. You know the boss when things ain't just right".

Jack Cunningham was still beating on the door of the telegraph office when Tom Larkin pulled it slowly open. Holding the lantern up, he peeked out through the small crack.

"Marshal Cunningham, you have any idea what time of night this is? I've got to open up in three hours".

"You're gonna' open up now Larkin. Get your pants on and get back in here. I got business and I ain't in no mood to fool with you. Now get movin'".

"Ain't nobody here but us marshal? I can send a telegram in my underwear as well as not. Write your message out there while I warm up the key".

When the message had been sent, Cunningham stepped

outside expecting to see Elk coming up the street with fresh
mounts. He waited a few minutes and then headed for the
livery. Elk was just getting to his feet when the marshal
stepped through the door with his pistol in his hand.
Elk saw him and staggered back, leaning against the stall
for support.
"You alright R.E.? What the hell happened"?
"Walked in on somebody. They must have heard me
coming and got the drop on me. Gone now".
Cunningham holstered his Dragoon and looked at his
friends head.
"Just the same that needs lookin' at. Better roll Doc Evans
out".
The groaning and thrashing from the one of the back stalls
caused both men to draw again and start in that direction.
Bill Allison had been hog tied and gagged and he was mad
as a hornet.
Elk helped the old timer to his feet and stepped back.
"Stand back son, I'm goin' after my shotgun! Ain't nobody
treats Bill Allison like no darned cow and gets away with it.
Get back boy! I'm comin' through".
Elk reached out and grabbed Bill's arm. "Now hold on Bill.
These people have mother and I need to know where
they're taking her".
The old man went wild. "You mean to tell me that these
varmints got Nancy? What in tarnation would they do a
thing like that for? That's it. I'm goin' for my gun. Get out
of the way son".
"Bill, near as I can tell, these people want mothers gold. I
need you to think now, and tell me if you heard anything.
It's important Bill".
The old man reached for his hat and began to pace back and
forth. "Come to think of it, they did say somethin' about a
feller named Mc. Somethin' or other. Said he should be real

happy with this haul. That help you any son"?

"More than you know Bill. Listen we'll need fresh mounts. Ours are done in after the ride back here from Lafayette. Three of em'. Jack will you get Oliver? He wants to be in on this, and we may need all the help we can get. Feels he's to blame for this and wants to make it right. I owe him that much".

"Right after you see the Doc. You ain't goin' to do anybody any good until you get patched up a little. Oliver's at the hotel. Pick us up there as soon as you're ready".

After Cunningham had left, Elk walked over and picked up his Winchester.

"Anything I can do son? I've known your Ma for quite a spell. I ain't done yet. Not by a long shot. Can still shoot and ride. Want me to come along"?

The young deputy walked over and put his hand on the old man's shoulder. "Bill, you were with my mother from the beginning. You and Zac both. If anything happened to you. I would never get over it. I may need you later, but for now. I need to go this alone".

"I understand son. If you need me, I'm here".

Doc Evans was waiting on Elk when he rode up. After having his scalp sewed back together, he thanked the Doc and headed for the hotel. Meeting Cunningham and Oliver at the hotel the three of them headed out the Smartsburg, Mace road toward Indianapolis.

"This is gettin' ugly R.E. This bunch grabbed your mother. Hog tied Bill and split your skull. Done all that in just one evening. Truth is, don't look like to me they care one way or the other if we know who they are. Got to be more to this than we can see".

"You may be right Jack. Dad, I don't have to tell you how serious this is. Is there anything you haven't told us"?

Oliver Stratton had gotten into something he couldn't begin

to handle. And right now all he wanted to do, was right a wrong. Nancy Weliever had been the best thing that had ever happened to him. He had gotten side tracked because of her money and whatever it took to make things right, he was going to do.

"Not that I can remember son. The games didn't even last that long. I'd go in and have a couple of drinks, and the next thing I know this fella is asking me to fill a chair. It all started out as fun. To tell you the truth, I was having a good time. Most times when I am on a job for the railroad, I'm by myself. The idea of having some fun for a change, sounded good to me. Things moved pretty fast after they got started. This fella by the name of McFarland sat in on the game and things changed for the worst. First thing I know I owe him over a thousand dollars and he say's my marker isn't any good and wants his money. I didn't have it and he has his boy's drag me out into the alley and beat me up. He came out and said if I didn't have his money by the end of the week he would go to the railroad and demand payment. I knew that would mean my job, so the only thing I could do was go to your mother for the money. That was the hardest thing I ever had to do in my life. Your mother and me have been married for almost twenty years now and I had to go to her with my tail between my legs and ask for help. I tell you, if I had it to do over again I would take another beating. Or even lose my job first".

Elk had been listening closely and at last had a clear picture of what had happened.

"Oliver, your only problem was getting involved with these people in the first place. You were dealing with professionals here. They saw you coming and set you up to get cleaned out. That happens all the time to unsuspecting folks. The thing took a wrong turn when you paid them in gold. Especially mothers gold. That's like throwing raw meat to a wolf. He's going to trail you right back to the source. That's what happened here. These people found out where you and mother lived and moved in".

Cunningham was listening to the conversation and forming some questions of his own. "The thing I don't understand yet, is what, does this dead fisherman have to do with what's goin' on now? These people are after the gold that's in the bank. Or that's the way it looks as of now. The rest of this gold is three thousand miles away. Stashed in some cave somewhere in the mountains of Wyoming. Some two bit gang in the Midwest doesn't have any hope of ever gettin' close to it. Or even know how much is there. How does it tie in"?

Oliver Stratton didn't look up, and his voice was strained when he spoke. "I'm to blame for that too. When they were beating me, McFarland kept asking me how much gold there was and where it came from. I finally told him your mother had been getting it for over fifteen years and it came from your father in Wyoming".

The muscles in Elk's jaw showed when he snapped his teeth together. Right then Oliver Stratton didn't want to see the anger in the young marshal's eyes.

A man never knows what he's made of until put to the test, and Oliver Stratton had failed miserably. The man had no backbone, even when it came to his wife's safety. He was a coward, and right now Elk hated him for it.

The three had passed Smartsburg and Mace and had just crossed Big Walnut Creek, and started up the bank when the bark on the maple tree exploded beside Elk's head. He rolled out of the saddle and came to his knees with his Colt in his hand. Cunningham had done the same, but Oliver hadn't moved as fast. The second shot had caught him in the right side of the chest and thrown him backward out of the saddle.

Things had happened so fast that it was a few seconds before the other two knew he had been hit. Cunningham was the first to see him.

"Elk, Oliver has been hit. Looks bad son".

Elk crawled over and looked down at the man who had spent all those years trying to be his father. The front of Oliver's shirt was covered with blood. Every time he breathed, bubbles would form around the wound. The young man pulled Oliver up and cradled him in his arms. There were tears in his eyes and he couldn't speak.

Oliver reached up and grabbed hold of the front of Elk's shirt. "Son, I'm so sorry".

Those were the last words he would ever say. Elk took out his handkerchief and wiped the blood from around Oliver's mouth. Laying him gently back down on the ground, he turned and disappeared into the woods.

When he returned, the knife his father had given him on his twelfth birthday was covered with blood. He walked to the creek and washed it off. "Jack, my father had this knife when he met my mother. It was part of his best outfit, and I have just used it to even the score for the man who raised me. Where is this goin' Jack"?

"I don't know son, but it's goin' to get worse before we get it straightened out".

Cunningham tied Oliver over the saddle of his horse, mounted his own and sat looking down at his young friend. "Elk. So far we got us two dead, and your mother kidnapped. We're headed back for Crawfordsville and I'm pullin' you off this. There are others who can track these people down just as well as you. After this, there ain't no way you're goin' to think straight. You bury Oliver, and leave the rest to me".

Elk pulled himself into the saddle and sat looking at the Captain. "The other man is about sixty yards off to the right. Take him back with you or leave him here. I don't care one way or the other. As for pullin' me off this. That could get real personal between us. I don't want it to come to that Jack. Do what you have to do, but from now on, stay out of my way until this is over. One other thing. Take this badge, I don't need it anymore. See you Jack".

Marshal Jack Cunningham sat and watched this young Indian head back toward Indianapolis and felt the cold chill of death start up his spine. He didn't like this, but it was exactly the reason he called on Richard Running Elk Weliever from time to time. "Lord I would hate to be on the other end of this". He rubbed Elk's badge on his vest and looked at for a minute. Slipped it into his pocket and headed back to see the undertaker in Crawfordsville.

Five

Elk headed up the road toward Jamestown a short way and pulled off to be sure he wasn't being followed. His old friend Cunningham was just starting back toward Crawfordsville with the two bodies. "Sorry Jack, but I had to deal you out of this one".

He hadn't told the marshal everything that had happened back at Big Walnut Creek. He sat there watching Cunningham work his way back toward town and wished he could have. But the man who had murdered Oliver had told him if he didn't come alone his mother would be killed. Oliver had just died in his arms and he had cornered the man before he could reach his horse. The killer had his rifle in his hands and heard Elk moving toward him. He turned to fire, recognized who was there and hesitated. That hesitation cost him his life.

In one fluid motion Elk moved his right hand up and pulled the big turquoise handled knife out of the sheath laying between his shoulders, brought his arm back down and let go of the knife in one motion. It flashed across the twenty feet of space separating the two and buried itself to the hilt in the man's stomach. He looked down at the beautiful inlaid handle and sank to his knees. Elk walked over to the man, bent down looked and into his eyes.

"Mister, you killed the man who raised me, and you have my mother. Why"?

Fear and death were on the strangers face, but he was a hard case. He spit blood at Elk.

"Go to hell half breed. I ain't tellin' you nothin'".

The knife was still in the man's belly and Elk admired his courage, but he needed information, and this man had it. He pulled the knife out and forced the man back down to the ground.

"You're dying mister. If you have something to say now's the time. Tell me what I want to know and I'll see you get a decent burial. Otherwise, I'll leave you out here for the birds and coyotes".

"It don't make no difference to me what you do. I ain't had no life anyway. Only thing I was supposed to do was let you know to come alone. Anybody else shows up and your Ma dies. I ain't sure but what Mac has already had some fun with her anyway".

Elk wanted to slit the man's throat but couldn't let his anger get the best of him. "How do I know where to find this Mac? Where is he"?

"Rena's place, Indianapo . . . "

The man's head fell back and was gone. The young marshal cleared his mind and formed his plan. Then headed back to where Cunningham was tying Oliver's body to his horse. Waiting until he could no longer see Cunningham and the horses, he turned and headed toward Jamestown and the Indianapolis road.

Arriving in Brownsburg sometime after midnight. His mount was tired and he needed time to get himself ready to meet what lay ahead. Making camp at Fletcher's pond he tended the horse, built a fire and began to make plans for the coming day. The young Indian sat before the fire long that night, thinking of his childhood and the times he had spent with Oliver. Whatever else the man had become. He had shown love to this boy and treated him as his own. He would not be forgotten.

To see the face of the young man riding into Indianapolis, this morning would cause one to step back into the shadows, out of the way.

Running Elk had risen early and bathed in the pond. When finished, he walked out of the water, picked up his white man's clothes, walked over to the fire and dropped them in.

He pulled his jet black hair back tight and tied it close, leaving the ends to fall down his back. Pulled on his native buckskins and moccasins. Ran the wide turquoise beaded belt through the sheath holding his knife and tied it around his waist. The last thing was to strap on the Colt and grab his Winchester.

It was another hour before he splashed across the shallows of White River and rode the short distance to Blake Street. Hearing laughter he turned his head in that direction. The eye's that looked out from under the straight brimmed hat left no doubt about this man's intent. The laughter subsided.

*Rena's place was located at the corner of New York and Indiana Avenue. Elk tied his horse to the lamppost and walked to the door, opened it and walked inside.

It took a few seconds for his eye's to adjust to the darkened interior of the place.

"Good morning sir. May I take your hat for you"?

Elk turned and looked at a black man dressed in a black uniform. He looked to be perhaps sixty, with an impeccably trimmed white beard.

He started to walk past the man. "No thanks, I'll just keep it. Don't plan to be here that long".

The doorman reached out and gently took hold of Elk's arm. The power in the old man's hand surprised him and he stopped.

"Sir, this is Rena's place and the rule is, no hats or guns in the inner rooms. I assure you sir, no one else is armed. You'll be quite safe. Your weapons please".

Elk wasn't quite sure why, but he trusted this old man. Unstrapping his gun belt he pulled the knife out of the sheath, and handed them over. "I'll be needing those in a bit".

"They will be right here sir. Who do you wish to see"?

"Let's start with Rena, and go from there".

"I'll see if she is in sir. Please make yourself comfortable".
While the doorman was gone, Elk had a look around. He had heard of places like this as a boy growing up in Crawfordsville, but this was his first time inside such a place.

It was magnificent. Carpeting that had to have been imported from around the world. With colors and designs of wild animals, and crowns covered in gold thread. The furniture looked to be hand carved of some exotic wood, and polished to a high luster. All of it covered in soft velvet. The plants that sat here and there were even potted in handmade woven baskets set in polished and engraved holders.

Back and off to the left was a huge staircase with steps covered in dark blue carpet. The rail was snow white and topped with what looked to be polished cherry. As his eyes followed the stairs upward, he could see beautiful murals and drapes that ran along the entire length of the balcony walls.

The doorman was standing at the far end talking to someone. He nodded his head and bowed slightly and then turned and came back down the stairs.

"Miss Rena will be along shortly sir".

Things weren't moving as fast as he would like, but this was his only lead and he had to play it by their rules. At least for now.

Hearing the door close, he turned to see a woman walking along the dimly lit corridor toward the stairs. It wasn't until she was about half way down that he had a good look at her.

She walked with such grace and charm, it made him feel uncomfortable to be in her presence.

The young man stood speechless as she approached. When she stopped in front of him and stuck out her hand. He was still unable to speak.

There before him stood the most beautiful woman he had ever seen. Dressed in an almost black red silk dress, trimmed in white lace, stood a woman who had the most beautiful smooth skin and brown eyes he had ever seen. When she smiled at him something happened to her face that made him want to look into her eyes. When she shook his hand, the touch of her set him on fire.

"Good morning sir. Please come into the guest room so we may talk in private". She turned and started off toward the back of the hall.

Elk followed without a word and tried as best he could to regain his composure. After they reached the guest room and were inside, the woman closed the door.

As beautiful as she was, it was plain she was all business. "This must be important sir. It is early for visitors. Also, your dress is most unusual for this part of the country. What do you want"?

The tone of her voice brought him back to the moment at hand and he began to talk. "Ma'am, you don't know me, and I sure don't know you. I need help, and you're the only name I've got. So here I am".

"I see. Well, let's get started off on the right foot shall we? First, I am not ma'am. My name is Rena Washington, and your name is"?

"I'm sorry, please excuse my manners. I'm Richard Running Elk Weliever Stratton. Deputy U.S.Marshal, I'm here to ask your help".

The young lady smiled as they shook hands again. "That's quite a name marshal. Do I use all of it, or can we settle on something shorter"?

In spite of the trouble he had to smile. "Folks just call me Elk, ma . . ., I mean Rena".

Rena turned and gestured to the small sofa behind her.

"Please sit down Elk. How can I help"?
"It's tough to know where to start. So I'll just tell you what's happened and perhaps you will have some suggestions as to where I should go from here".

Elk started in and when he finished the woman had her hand over her mouth and tears on her cheeks. "I'm sorry Rena, but I have no other place to go, but to you. This is rough business and I don't know the city, or the area around here for that matter. Do you know where I can find this McFarland? He seems to be the answer to my mother's whereabouts".

The young woman reached out and took his hand. "I know of this McFarland. He is a gambler and troublemaker. Perhaps, even worse. He has been here on occasion and I believe I can find him. It may take a little time, but I will try".

Elk stood up to leave. "Thank you. We don't have a lot of time. I'm sure he wants my mother's gold and whatever else he can get. Can you tell me of a place where I can get a room for a few days? I need to get some clothes that don't stand out too much, and I'll have to find a place to board my horse".

Rena got up and walked to the door and called the doorman over. "Mr. Franklin, this is Marshal Running Elk. He will be staying with us for a few days. Please show him to the guest room at the top of the stairs and see to his horse. This afternoon I want you to take him to Cooper's tailor shop and have Mr. Cooper see to his needs. I will see you at supper Elk, if we are to find this man. I must get busy. "

Elk began to object, but the doorman cut him off. "Marshal, This young lady runs this place. It's hers, left to her by her dear departed father. If she wants to do something, nothing, you can say will make any difference. Please come along sir".

On the way up the stairs, Elk looked over at the man. "Mr. Franklin, I was raised by a woman who was strong willed like Rena. Got used to it early. No use in tryin to change their minds once they get set on something. It is very nice of her to take me in like this. Don't really know what to say".

"She is a wonderful lady sir. And you're quite right. She is very beautiful. Here's your room sir. I will be by directly and escort you to the tailor. Will that be all sir"?

"Nope, one more thing".

"Yes sir"?

"Call me Elk".

The man smiled and stuck out his hand. "And my name is Thaddeus Brewster Franklin. Be back in about an hour".

*At the turn of the century, there were many places such as Rena's. Though the name is fiction. The local, and street names are not. These were grand places to spend an evening out. Visitors came to this area of Indianapolis from all over the country, to dine and watch plays, and listen to the latest in music. Women in beautiful evening gowns escorted by men dressed just as elegantly, arrived in horse drawn carriage. It was a time of romance and excitement. The big cities in the east, or west for that matter, had nothing with more splendor than those in Indianapolis.

Six

The two hours Elk spent at the tailors seemed like an eternity. His mother had been kidnapped and was even now being abused as far as he knew. He hadn't been contacted by anyone and to make matters worse, Miss Rena hadn't returned with any news of McFarland.

He left the tailor shop and headed down the Avenue toward the center of town. As he waited for the beer wagon to pull out of the alley, he heard someone call out.

"Hey Indian".

Elk slipped off the tether holding the hammer on his Colt and walked into the alley. It took a minute to adjust his eyes to the deep shadows between the buildings. He could hear talking and laughter ahead, but it was further up the alley.

"Over here Indian".

Elk followed the voice and stepped around the corner of the nearest building and found himself facing a well dressed man of about thirty. He smelled of cologne and soap, and Elk noticed he was standing on newspaper to keep his shoes from getting dirty.

"What do you want mister"?

"First thing is, don't go for that cannon there, or I don't say nothin' and your mother dies".

Elk reached out with both hands, grabbed the man's coat front and spun him around. Forcing him against the wall, he smashed his face into the rough bricks several times, and then turned him back around.

The man's nose was broken and blood had begun to run down his suit front. Elk backhanded the man and his head popped back against the wall. He fell forward in a heap at Elk's feet gagging and spitting blood. The Indian pulled his knife, and reaching down, jerked the man to his feet. The fear in the man's eyes told Elk all he needed to know about the fight left in him. He laid the ten inch blade against the man's cheek and began to speak.

"As you can tell, I'm not a patient man. If I didn't need information from you I would cut your throat right now and leave you here in the mud where you belong. You get one chance with me mister, and this is it. Where are you holding my mother"?

The man's eyes were glued to the knife in Elk's hand. He shivered and could feel the warmth running down his leg, the breath caught in his throat. Elk's grip tightened on the man's shirtfront.

"Mister, you're going to do more than piss your pants if I have to wait any longer. For the last time. Where are you holding my mother"?

"My God mister! What's the matter with you? I'm just supposed to give you a message. I don't know nothin' about your mother, honest. I just said that to scare you. Just a message, that's all I got. Just a message".

Elk released the man and took a step back. "Sorry, I guess I'm not used to the way you folks do things here. What's the message"?

"You're to go to the lobby at the Strand Hotel and leave the information about the location of the rest of it with the desk clerk. I'm to tell you your mother is OK for now, but if you don't do as you're told. She will die".

Elk almost hated to ask the next question. "The rest of what"?

"They said you would know. Please let me go mister. All I do is run errands for people. That's how I get by. You know how it is".

"Do you know how to get back to these people who sent you after me"?

"I'm supposed to meet a man at Morgan's Bar as soon as I leave here. Wants to know how you took the message. He gets a look at me and he'll know how you took it. I only got one other suit mister, you owe me fifteen dollars for this suit".

"What's your name"?

"Glen Hightower. Why"?

"Well Glen Hightower, you're now working for me. I'm going to give you fifteen dollars and you're going to lead me to this man at Morgan's Bar. You got that"?

"I can't do that! They will kill me for sure. I don't want your money mister. Just let me go".

"It's them or me. Take your choice".

Glen looked at the knife in Elk's hand. "Don't follow too close".

"I'm going to give you a half a block head start. If you run, I will chase you and I will catch you. Do you understand?'

"Mister Indian, I've had enough of you to last me a lifetime. Where's the money"?

"Elk pulled a twenty dollar gold piece out of his pocked and handed it to the man".

"Get moving".

It was almost dark when the man walked into the bar. Elk waited about fifteen seconds and followed him in. Any longer, and it would have been too late. As it was, the man seated at the far end of the bar was already getting off his stool and heading for the back door.

The place was crowded with customers having a drink on their way home from work, and there was no way for him to get to the man before he reached the door. He did the only thing he could do.

The big Colt jumped in his hand and the heavy slug slammed into the wall beside the man's head.

Reaction from the customers in the bar wasn't what he

expected. These folks were flatlanders and not used to gunplay. Women were screaming and men were diving for the floor. There was less chance now to get the man than there was before.

Elk started after the man anyway only to feel the hard steel of a revolver in his ribs. He turned toward the pain and found himself looking at a badge pinned on the chest of the local police.

The face of the man belonging to the badge was not smiling.

"Mister, I don't know where you're from, but you're in Indianapolis now, and we don't draw down on people around here. I want you to reach out real slow and lay your pistol on the table there in front of you. Make a wrong move now lad, and today will be your last day".

Elk was mad, he was in a bind here and he knew it.

"I'm U.S. Deputy Marshal Richard Running Elk Weliever Stratton. Here on official business and I'm after that man back there".

As he pointed toward the back of the room, he saw the man smile and step through the door.

"Is that right lad? Well looks like we may have spoiled things for you. Let me see your badge and we can get this cleared up right now. Not that we need shooting in a public place mind you".

Elk reached inside his vest to the pocket he kept his badge in and remembered he had given it to Jack Cunningham.

"Sorry men, I seemed to have misplaced it".

"I see, well now that does pose a problem. Dale, perhaps you would be good enough to put this man in cuffs. Mr. Richard whoever you are. You're under arrest".

It was midnight before the telegram from Cunningham arrived and the door was opened to Elk's cell. He picked up his weapons and started for the door.

"Marshal. Just a word of advice. Don't start shooting up our city. Marshal or no, next time, your boss will have to come down here and get you out himself".

Elk nodded and stepped through the door. The three miles he walked to get back to Rena's place gave him time to plan his next move.

Rena's was closed, but the doorman was waiting for him. He let him in, said goodnight and stepped back outside.

He was about to head to his room when Rena Washington stepped from the shadows that had overtaken the hall and startled him. "Well Elk, you certainly do get things stirred up. Come, I have some news for you".

Everything he had done today seemed to have been wrong. To involve this woman in his trouble could get her and anyone close to her hurt, or worse. He wasn't going to let that happen.

"Rena, this is bad business. I don't seem to be making any headway here, and I don't want to get you involved. I don't even know why you're helping me".

"Elk several years ago some of my people were trying to leave the south. They were being chased and some were caught and hanged. Others made it a little further and were caught and sent back. Some, the very lucky ones found help from people who cared. Four in particular were sent to a very fine lady who fought their battle and took them to safety. She drove a huge team of mules and carried a ten gauge scattergun. The name of the man she helped was Washington. He had a wife and two little girls with him. That man was my father Elk. The woman who helped him was your mother. I will never forget that ride. Or, the woman who fought like a tiger, against all odds to get us to safety. I, and my people would lay our lives down for her. So don't be concerned about us. We know how to find these people and we will help".

The young woman began to tell of that trip north with his mother so many years ago. Of the gunplay, and the speed of the mules. Of the giant dog, that was always by his mother's side. Or of the woman from Georgia, and the showdown between the two that could have been in any frontier town in the west.

"We watched as she walked out alone for that showdown Elk, alone! She was facing a rifle and death was at hand, I will never forget that brave woman as long as I live".

The sky was turning light before Elk drifted off to sleep with his mother's face in his mind. He would find her, and there would be hell to pay along the way.

Seven

Elk hadn't been asleep an hour when he was awakened by the cold tip of a pistol at his temple. He opened his eyes and reached for the lamp, but the pressure of the gun at his head increased.

"Marshal, If, I have to kill you, I will. Make no mistake about that at all. What I want you to do is keep your mouth shut and listen. First off. Considering the situation your mother is in, you're being very hard headed. If you keep that up, we will kill her and be done with it. Gold or no gold. This is a business with us and we're good at it. So you have a decision to make.

Second, if you want her to be returned to you. You will turn over the gold to us. All of it. And give us the information we need, to find where the rest of it is stored. You do all of that, and we give her back to you. Simple business matter, nothing else. Your answer to the following question will determine what we do next. Will you do business with us"?

Elk could see he was dealing with an educated man. That at least was some progress. It also made the situation more dangerous. His decision was a simple one.

"When and where"?

The man patted his shoulder. "That wasn't hard at all. Was it? The information you need is on the nightstand. Follow it, and by this time tomorrow, your mother will be home safe and sound".

The cold steel pressed against his head was removed and he could hear the man moving toward the door. He rose up on one elbow and looked in that direction.

"Friend".

"Yes".

"If this goes wrong and something happens to my mother. There will be no place on earth you will be able to hide. It

is said that my people can track a ghost through the treetops. I am better than that".
He heard the man laugh.
"I bet you are at that".
Rolling out of bed, he lit the lamp and reached for the note. It told him where and when the gold was to be delivered. Elk dressed and headed for the telegraph office.
The office ran twenty four hours a day in the city. He scribbled a brief message to Jack Cunningham, writing him to pull the gold out of the bank and bring it to Indianapolis. The message raised the eyebrows of the clerk.
He rode out meeting Cunningham on the Liston road and it was sometime after noon when they crossed White River and headed toward the north side of town. Once they passed the stockyards the country began to open up somewhat.
"You just going to turn this box of gold over to these people Elk? There must be over a hundred thousand dollars here son".
"If that's what it takes Jack. I don't care about the money. These people are talking about my father's people now. I'm not going to let it go that far".
"Where we supposed to meet em'. I don't know this country through here".
"Place called Eagles Nest Creek. There have been three of em' following us since we left town. I'm not riding into this thing blind Jack. May have a talk with them directly".
"Might not be a bad idea at that. What do you want to do about these boys following us"?
"Nothing right now. May need em' later. Funny what you white folks will do for money Jack. This has turned into a hell of a mess".
"Can't argue that point with you R.E. I've been a lawman all my life and know for sure I won't ever see this kind of

money. Who says crime don't pay"?

"Uh, huh. The pay day at the end of this road isn't going to be what they expect".

They rode on quietly for another hour keeping track of the riders behind them and on the road ahead. Rounding a bend, they spotted a youngster sitting on his pony in the middle of the road.

"Reckon that'll be the information we been looking for R.E. I just had a look at our back trail and those three are a bit closer than they should be. Things could get a might pinched here".

"Don't care anymore. I'm in no mood for any of this. They want to mix, let's mix, the hell with it".

"Hang on R.E. We need to get to Nancy. Gunplay right now ain't goin to help anybody. Let's keep a cool head for now. We need this kid to give us information. When we have it that might be a different story. Better let me do the talkin".

The young man nodded, but reached over and slid the tether off the hammer on his Colt anyway. Cunningham saw the move and did the same.

"Damn R.E., I sure would hate to have you on my case. You're mean as a snake. No wonder I get you involved in this stuff. I'd almost forgotten how you get once you're on a trail".

Cunningham pulled the wagon to a stop about twenty feet from where the youngster sat his horse and waited. The boy road his pony up and stopped beside the wagon looking Elk over.

"Mister. Are you the Indian they told me to look for"?

Elk smiled at the young man, reached behind his neck and pulled out the ten inch blade that had been resting there.

"Young man, suppose you and I have us a talk".

"Mister. You ain't goin' to cut me. You ain't that kind. You ride on up ahead about two miles and take the first road to the west. Someone will meet you on the bridge this side of the creek. Ain't never seen no Indian before. They all as friendly as you? Kneeing his pony and started back down the road. Elk watched him for a second, slid the blade back into the sheath and turned to look at Cunningham.

"Well R.E. that just impressed the hell out of me. My, but you do have a way with folks. Real glad you didn't want nothin' else out of that youngster, you'd have to run him down".

The young marshal nodded. "Yeah, well suppose we just go and have a talk with this person that's supposed to meet us on the bridge. Another thing, I want to move slowly enough that those three behind will catch up a little. We need to clean that up before we get too much further on. As soon as we round that bend up ahead there, you swing to the right and I'll swing left and we'll just ease up behind them".

"Good enough. I been a little nervous about that anyway. Just as well cut the odds down a might".

When the three that had been following rounded the bend, the two marshals stepped out into the road with guns drawn and stopped them. Cunningham spoke first. "Just set easy there gentlemen and you might live through this. As you can see by the badge I'm wearing here I can shoot you and it will be all legal like. Who are you and who are you workin' for"?

"Go to hell, marshal. We ain't tellin' you nothin'. Besides you got no right stoppin' us, all we was doin was ridin' along same as you. Now get the hell out of the way and let us pass".

The man nudged his horse as if to ride on only to have Elk reach up and grabbed the reins. "You don't have to ask who they are working for Jack. Look at those hats their wearing.

Look like soup bowls to me. These boys are working for McFarland".

Cunningham nodded and walked around in front of the three. "You boys got two choices. You can run, in which case me and my deputy here will be obliged to gun you down. Or you can get your asses off them horses and down on the ground, and I mean right now! What's it going to be boys"?

The three climbed down off their horses and Cunningham walked them across the road and sat them down with their backs up against a tree. He tied a rope around the tree and under the chin of each one just tight enough so if one moved much, the other two would choke. When that was done, he took the reins of their mounts and he and Elk headed for their own. They hadn't gone ten steps when one of them sang out.

"Come on, marshal. You just can't just leave us here like this. How we gonna' get back"?

"Back where mister"?

"Chicago. We're from Chicago. We borrowed these horses in Indianapolis".

"Uh huh. I'll just bet your boss is real proud of you right about now. Tell you what. It's about ten or twelve miles to Indianapolis, and I reckon about two hundred to Chicago. You boys will get loose there directly and it would be a good idea if you lit out for home. I ever see any of you again and I'll send you home by train, in a box". The two lawmen mounted up and rode on up the road. "Where the hell, do these people come from R.E.? Don't anybody want to work for a living anymore? Never mind. I reckon if they did you and me wouldn't have nothin to do".

Eight

The barn set close enough to Eagle Creek that Nancy could hear the creek, and see through the broken window they were in the country somewhere. She had been tied to the chair in this same position for most of the day, and her muscles were beginning to cramp. If she was going to make a move to escape, it would have to be soon. Night would give her the best cover for escape.

She had a plan, and now was as good a time as any to put it into action. McFarland had been gone for about half an hour and had left the two that had taken her in charge until he returned. To the man's credit he had told them she was not to be harmed. At least until they got what they wanted from Elk. Nancy knew in the situation she was now in, he would be coming with the gold. She also knew once these men had it, there would be no reason to keep her or Elk alive. They would simply kill them, ride off, and no one would be the wiser.

The two were standing at the barn door smoking and talking. She readied herself and called out.

"Hey you two. How about letting a lady relieve herself. You two have done it at least twice since we've been here".

They finished their smokes and ground the butts out under the heels of their boots and walked over.

She could smell the big one's breath from three feet away. He reached out and tilted her head back and leaned in close. "What's the matter lady? Can't hold it huh? What's it worth to let you go? How's this for a start"?

The man leaned closer and kissed her square on the mouth. The stench of his breath and the taste of his rotting teeth filled her mouth. Her stomach turned, and the temptation to bite off his bottom lip was almost more than she could bear, but she didn't move. Vomit began to work its way to her throat, but this to she fought back. The man straightened up and looked down at her.

"That wasn't so bad, now was it? Smith. I think we got us a winner here. What say you and I have us a little fun, right now? She's tied to the chair. What can she do"? Max stepped forward and straddled the chair and unbuttoned the front of his trousers.

If Nancy was going to do anything at all, it would have to be now. She smiled at the man.

"Max. I've been setting here all day. Don't you think this would be more fun if I could be part of this? What can I do? We're out here in the middle of nowhere. Where could I go? There are two of you. What about Mr. Smith there? Mr. Smith you're going to get in on this to, aren't you? Untie me so I can relieve myself and get straightened up a little. Then we can have a good time. After all, what McFarland don't know won't hurt him, will it".

The men looked at each other and smiled. Max nodded, and Smith came over and untied her. Nancy sat for a few seconds and rubbed her wrist to bring back the circulation. She was stiff and sore from setting all day, and her shoulder hurt badly from the cuts she had received while riding in the wagon. That would all have to be blocked out of her mind if this was to work. There would be only one chance, and if it failed, there was no doubt about the outcome. Max reached out, and roughly jerked her to her feet. "You get done what you need to get done and get back in here. Smith is goin' along to see to that. You try anything and when we get through with you your husband won't even want you. You hear what I say lady"?

Nancy nodded and looked around. Her plan had already been made, and now was as good as time as any to get the ball rolling. She took a first step and could feel her body react to the abuse she had received. The first step caused excruciating pain to shoot up her right leg and into her hip. The beating and wagon ride had taken their toll. What she wouldn't give to be thirty-five again, but that was a thing of the past. She swallowed the pain and moved toward the door, put her hand on the handle and pushed it open. Cool air greeted her and she breathed it in welcoming her moment of freedom, however brief.

Walking toward Eagle Creek she spotted a small group of low growing bushes she could hear Smith on her heels. If this was going to work, she would have to at least get him to leave her alone for a few seconds. It was a poor ploy, but right now, she was grasping for anything she could get. Slowing a bit she waited until he was very close and then squatted right in front of him. Turning, she looked at the man and acted as surprised as she could. She stood up quickly and pulled her dress back down. "Mr. Smith as you can see I am not going anywhere near the water's edge. Could you at least afford a lady a small bit of privacy"? The man looked at her and smiled showing green rotting teeth. "No deal lady. You heard what Max said. I was to keep an eye on you. Now get back down there and do your business and be quick about it, or I'll drag you back in there and we'll go at it anyway".

This was her only chance and she had to do something else and quick if this was going to work. She reached down and grabbed the bottom of her dress and in one quick motion pulled it up and over the top of her head and off. She handed it to Smith and smiled. Seeing he was surprised she pressed the point. "Mr. Smith, do you honestly think I am going anywhere with no clothes on but my drawers? Please give me a moment's privacy to take care of my business. You can do that can't you"?

Max had become impatient and stepped to the barn door. "Smith! What the hell you doin' out there. We're supposed to share her. Get her done and get your ass back in here before I come out there"!

Smith looked back to see if Max could see them. Satisfied

he couldn't, he made his decision. "Okay lady. You got one minute. Get your business done and be quick about it". He backed up four or five paces and turned around.

Nancy smiled at the man and started around behind the bushes. "Thank you Mr. Smith, I won't be long. Would you stay close to me when we return? I really don't want Max to touch me right off. He's so dirty".

Smith smiled at her words and let his imagination begin work. "Be glad to hold your hand lady, Max will just have to wait his turn. You know, I ain't new at this. Had me a woman once. Well, a girl really, fifteen or sixteen maybe. Died on me though, think I squeezed her too hard. Didn't want to get in no trouble so I dug a hole in the side of the hill and buried her. Didn't leave no marker or nothin', spect' she's still there. You bout' done lady? We better get back now". He took another half step back and turned again to see if Max was coming to check on them. He turned back just in time to catch the full force of a three foot by two inch piece of driftwood right in the face. The blow lifted him off his feet and he landed on his back and lay still. Nancy leaned over, picked up her dress, and relieved him of his revolver. Slipped her dress back over her head and stepped into Eagle Creek heading for the opposite bank and the road home. There was a score to settle and she aimed to do just that. Besides, someone was going to answer for the legs being blown off her kitchen table. She also decided she was going to settle the score with Max.

Nine

McFarland had left the barn and gone on to the bridge. He knew Elk would be coming for his mother and as he settled down to wait it was a grim and evil smile he was wearing. He had been in this business for a long while and it always turned out the same. Try as he might he was never able to understand why people were so easy to manipulate. Unlike those, he knew it seemed whenever his kind put pressure on other folks for money they always caved in as if it meant nothing. Shaking his head in thought he moved back into the brush, rolled a cigarette, lit it and threw the match into the creek. He would be able to hear the horses coming up the road so he pulled his hat over his eyes and settled back to wait.

Elk and Cunningham had made the turn to the west as the youngster had instructed and had gone about a mile or so when the bridge came into view about three hundred yards ahead. Cunningham motioned the young marshal to take to the tree line to keep him out of site and pulled the wagon to a stop. Taking a small spyglass out of a leather pouch he had secured to his belt, he extended it and scanned the area on both sides of the road looking for movement.

Seeing none, he put the scope back in the case and without turning his head began to speak. "Don't see nothin" R.E. Course, that don't mean they ain't there. Most likely hidin' in the brush somewhere".

"Uh huh. They're not expecting anyone but me. Reckon I'll go on alone from here. I aim to come out of there with my mother alive Jack so I need to do as they said. I'll take the wagon and leave my Colt with you".

Cunningham looked at his young friend and nodded his agreement. "One thing R.E. You know if you go in there alone with this gold, there ain't a reason in the world for them not to kill you. Think about it son. They already have the whereabouts of the gold your father knows about. Hell, they are most likely on the way to it right now. The only reason they took Nancy was out of greed. You know as well as I do that's the whole thing with their kind. They got to have it all, and it's got to be their way. What we got to do, is beat them at their own game. Now think on this a minute. For all we know someone could be watchin' us right now, so you get on this here wagon and put my hat on, at this distance they won't never know the difference. You drive the wagon on ahead slow like so I can keep up by walking just inside the tree line there and if we come up on somebody lookin' to bushwhack you, I will be able to surprise em'. If not, things can go as you say and no one will be the wiser"

Elk liked the plan and swung down off his horse. Unbuckled his gunbelt and handed it to Cunningham. He also untied his knife and slipped into the back of his trousers then reached for the marshal's hat. As he spoke to his old friend, the look in his eyes was cold and hard. "Jack if they have hurt mother, I want you to turn and walk away. There may be a score to settle, and if need be I will do it right in front of you and to hell with the law".
Cunningham nodded. "I got your back son. Go do what you have to do".
Elk started the wagon rolling toward the bridge again keeping the pace slow so the marshal could side him from the cover of the trees.
McFarland was on his third smoke when the harness leather creaking when the wagon was about a hundred yards from the bridge alerted him. He flipped his smoke into the creek and reached up under his coat pulling a small pistol.
Thinking to himself how easy this was going to be he moved just enough to be able to ambush Elk with one clear shot. He took his hat off and laid it carefully out of the way

so as not to get it soiled. Drew in his breath and let it out slowly to steady his hand, eased the hammer back and took dead aim on the young marshal's chest.

Nancy had just gotten across the creek and started up the far bank when she smelled cigarette smoke. Keeping to the bank she eased her way along until she found a break in the brush, it was then what she remembered what her old friend Zacaria Farley had told her about hunting prey. "Nancy if you watch a cat catch a mouse, or a fox huntin' a rabbit they always stay on their belly until the last minute. Then when they jump they are close enough to get the job done. So if you are huntin', do the same thing. We can learn a lot from critters". In spite of the danger she had to smile at her memory of the old man. At the same time she went on her belly and began to ease up the bank in the direction of the smoke.

Elk and Cunningham were easing along toward the bridge unaware of the danger the young marshal was in. The bullet in McFarland's pistol had been hollowed out on the tip. He was an evil man and after every kill would take the time to examine the body of his victim. These hollow tip bullets made a very small hole going in, but when they came out there was often a wound the size of a man's hand. If the victim was unlucky enough not to die instantly, the pain was unbearable. McFarland liked to watch his victims suffer. Just now he was squeezing the trigger that would send the bullet hurtling toward Elks chest ending this young man's life. He squeezed the trigger and felt the pistol buck in his hand.

Cunningham heard the shot and turned toward Elk. The wagon seat where he had been just seconds before was empty. The sudden report from McFarland's pistol had startled the team and they had bolted ahead toward the bridge. He waited until his view was clear and with pistol drawn, stepped out into the road. Bushwhackers and back shooters had always angered him because they were not only outlaws, but cowards to boot. Rage welled up in the marshal and he yelled out. "You dirty sons of bitches! Step out here and let's see what you're made of damn you! Filthy cowards! Bastards, all of you"! His words were interrupted by his young friend. "Damn Jack. You're getting' a might worked up, ain't you? Didn't know you cared so much".

Cunningham turned and looked in the ditch where Elk had landed when he had rolled out of the seat just seconds before. The marshal ran over and squatted down by his young friend. "Hi pard. Thought they had got you for sure. You see where the shot came from? Damn it R.E. why didn't you holler at me. I could have been shot standin' out there in the road like that"?

Elk smiled at the older man. "I was going to, but when you went into action like that I was so impressed I just wanted to watch for a minute. Haven't seen you that wound up since you played that trombone of yours at Sue Ellen's wedding, of course you were a might well-oiled right then. Now that I think on it you might consider quitting this lawman business and starting your own band.

"Aw shut up and get out of the ditch. This is serious business here and you're yappin' like a drunken sailor. My God R.E., we got work to do here".

"You're right. Sorry Jack. I saw movement in the brush ahead and to the left about thirty yards just before the shot. Got to think whoever it was is gone or they would have been on us by now. Let's get back across the road and we can flush em' out if their still there. Got to do something, the team is clear on the other side of the bridge. Think you can make it back across the road there without getting so dramatic"?

"Lord. I hate it when you're like this. Why is it whenever we're in this kind of scrape you start your foolin' around?

My God R.E. you could be dead right now". "Who knows? Let's have a look around. And no yelling". The two crossed the road on a run, slipped into the tree line, and began moving toward the spot where the shot had come from.

Max had waited as long as he dare, and started out to bring Smith and Nancy back to the barn. He was angered at the thought of being left out of the fun and called out. "Smith. Damn you! If you're already on that woman, I'm goin' to make you mighty sorry! You know McFarland's comin' back. Get off her and get back here. Where are you anyway"? He rounded the brush where the two had been to find Smith sitting on the ground holding his bloodied face in his hands. Max looked quickly around and knew what had happened. "Where's the woman"? Smith didn't answer and he became enraged. He grabbed the man by the head, jerked him off the ground and threw him into the creek. Smith landed on his back and rolled over and got to his knees trying to get up "You worthless piece of shit! You let her get away! He kicked the downed man in the side of the head causing him to fall into the water. Kicked him again, and turned him face down in the water, put his foot on the back of his neck holding him under. "You son of a bitch! Damn you! You got any idea what McFarland is goin to do to me when he finds out the woman is gone"?

Smith was struggling and trying to get air, but he couldn't get his head above water. He could hear Max saying something, but it wasn't clear. His lungs were bursting and he was begging to be let up. Things seem to go into slow motion then and he began to relax and then all was black and he was gone.

Max had been raving about letting the woman escape and didn't realize Smith had stopped struggling until the foot he had been holding him under with began to get wet. He looked at the man floating in the water and when he began to move downstream, turned and headed back toward the barn.

Nancy had come up out of the water on her belly and began to inch her way through the mud toward where she thought the smoke was coming from. She knew this would be McFarland and there wasn't a doubt in her mind of his intentions toward Elk. She took several handfuls of mud and rubbed it on her face and arms as best she could to keep the sun from reflecting off her skin, then started up the bank. She chanced a look over the top just in time to see McFarland move to one side and take a deep breath, let it out and aim the pistol he was holding toward the road. She had to do something quickly or it would be too late. She reached over and picked up a fallen branch a little over two feet long, went over the bank and was on McFarland before he realized it. She placed the branch under his chin and pulled him backward toward her. As he was coming down she put both legs over the branch behind her knees and crossed her legs at the ankles in the middle of his back. Leaning backward as far as she could, she forced the branch into McFarland's throat.

McFarland had been concentrating on Elks chest and had not heard Nancy come over the bank. When the branch had been put to his throat, surprise had made his hand squeeze the trigger and the shot had gone wild. The shock of the bullet being fired had made the pistol jump from his hand and he found himself pinned between Nancy and the branch under his throat. His air was cut off and he knew if he didn't get loose quick he would strangle Reaching back as far as he could he was able to grab one of her breasts. Before he could hurt her, she knocked his hand away. "Keep your hands to yourself pig. You don't know me that well". Realizing who it was that had him. He began thrashing around and swearing. His words were not more than a rasp coming through his clenched teeth.

"You bitch I'll kill you"!
Nancy responded in kind. "Not in this lifetime you piece of crap. How's this for leg pressure from a lady? By the way. Are you responsible for breaking my kitchen table"?
Spittle had started to drip from McFarland's mouth, and he began to relax from the lack of air. Nancy gave one final jerk with her legs and heard his neck snap from the pressure. Unwinding herself from the dead man she got to her feet.
Elk and Cunningham had been coming through the brush with guns at the ready. They stepped into the clearing just in time to hear the bones snap in McFarland's neck.
Cunningham grimaced and shivered a bit. "God I hate that sound". The two stood and watched in amazement as Nancy let the man drop to the ground and got up. She looked at her son and smiled.
"Don't look so surprised Richard. I didn't live this long and raise you by being weak. It was either him or you, and I made a choice".
Elk smiled at her and walked over and gave her a hug.
"You don't have to explain anything to me mother. Father didn't choose you because you were like all the rest. C'mon, let's get you cleaned up and get out of here".
"Not just yet. There is one more thing I have to do".
Leaving out some of the details she pointed to the barn and told them of Max and his friend Smith.
Marshal Cunningham nodded his understanding and after they had removed the body of McFarland he and Elk started across the bridge to round up the other two. They spotted Smiths body near the far bank. It had caught on an exposed tree root and was bobbing up and down like a cork. They hauled it back up to the road and threw it in the wagon. "Funny how things work, ain't it RE.? This man's boss tries to kill you and this wagon stops just at the right place for us to load a body. Tell you what son. It just don't

pay to be mean". Cunningham looked back across the bridge and saw Nancy coming and shook his head. His face showed grim concern. "You reckon she did this too"? "No. Don't think so. She still thinks there are two of them over there".

Cunningham until Nancy got to them and reached over and picked up a piece of rolled up canvas and pulled out her scatter gun. "Picked this up off your kitchen floor. Thought you might want it".

She thanked him and cradled the double barrel in her left arm.

Elk thought his mother had seen about all the action she needed for one day. He took the canvas Jack had brought and walked over and spread it out under an old maple tree that wasn't more than ten feet from the wagon. "Mother, me and Jack are goin' over and flush out the last one. I don't want to leave you alone with this body, but I don't want you going over there either. There might be gunplay and you have had a long couple of days".

She nodded in agreement and sat down, leaning her back up against the tree. I am a little bushed Richard. Don't be long".

Max had returned to the barn and decided he didn't want to deal with McFarland. He knew the man would kill him sure as not and he began saddling his horse preparing to leave. He was about to swing into the saddle when the two marshals stepped through the barn door and faced him. Neither man had touched their pistols as yet, it was plain Max didn't want them to. Elk stepped forward a step or two. "You the piece of shit that roughed up my mother"? He reached behind his back and pulled the ten inch blade from his trousers. Cunningham saw his intent and stepped in front of him.

The eye's he was looking in to, were hard and unforgiving. He had seen Elk like this before and knew he was on dangerous ground. "We ain't goin' to do this thing R.E. This part of the fight is over and I aim to take this man back to jail. He'll die, but the law will do it. I'd be obliged if you put that sticker up and we did this like the lawman we are". The young marshal was looking past his old friend at Max with unflinching eyes. Cunningham reached over and laid his hand on Elks arm and felt coiled steel. He had a job to do here and knew if his young friend went through with this thing the law would be compromised. He was not going to let this go that far.

"You son of a bitch! Step away from that horse"! Elk started past Cunningham and the marshal threw both arms around him pinned his arms to his sides. It was a useless effort. He was brushed aside like a evening nat. "Get off me! Jack! I got a score to settle here and you're in the way. If you don't want to see it, step outside. Damn it Jack! Get the hell out of the way"!

The marshal shook his head and once again stepped in front of his friend. "R.E., I've known you almost all your life. Hell. I love you like you was my own son, but you try to do this thing and I'll arrest you sure. I'm sworn to uphold the law Elk. You know that for God's sake! Don't put me in that spot". It was then that marshal Cunningham pulled his dragoon and aimed it at Max's heart. "You ain't going to do this thing Elk! I'll kill this son of a bitch myself! I swear it"!

"You're not going to be put in any spot marshal. I was the one brought here and I will be the one to decide this man's fate".

The three men turned to see Nancy standing in the barn door holding her scatter gun at the ready. She was covered from head to toe with drying mud. It was caked in her hair and on her dress. Her shoes were full of mud and spots of it had begun to dry on her legs.

Elk looked at Cunningham and smiled. The marshal was

looking at Nancy and his body was shaking all over from laughter. He was trying not to be loud, but the site of Nancy standing there was too much for him. His head began to bob up and down as he laughed and he finally lost control and began to roar with laughter. It was contagious and Elk began to laugh as well. Even Max was smiling, although he wasn't sure why.

Nancy got mad. "Well! You two think this is funny do you! How would you like to be standing here with mud all over you? Look at Max over there. He even thinks this is funny". She walked over and picked up a well used grooming brush off of a bench in the tack area and came back and stood in front of Max and held it out to him. "Max. A while back you got a little too close to me and I noticed you smelled bad. Real bad. I don't want to have to smell you all the way back to town, so you are going to take a bath". She handed the stiff bristled brush to him and marched him out of the barn toward the creek threatening to shoot him if he didn't do as she said. The two men followed her and Max through the door. They could see her hair was caked with mud and stuck to the back of her neck. There was a small stick stuck to the right side of her head and one of her stockings was falling down over one shoe. Elk again chanced a look at Cunningham. The marshal was having a little trouble breathing and there were tears running down his cheeks. "Damn Jack, you do get tickled don't you? We got two dead bodies here and you're laughing. Get hold of yourself. Can't you see mother's mad? You don't mess with mother when she's mad. Straighten up"!

"I'm trying R.E. give me a minute".

Nancy had Max strip and prodded him into the cold water with the point of her scatter gun. She reached out and handed him the brush. "Get to scrubbing, Max. Rub hard. You got a lot of stink to get off. Max began to scrub with the rough brush and everywhere it touched his skin turned red. Nancy stood and watched for a minute and turned to Elk. "You boys watch him for me. I'm going down stream a ways and see if I can get some of this mud off me. Look at Max. No wonder he has a hard time with the ladies. His tool is about the size of a small radish".

She walked away and Elk turned back to find Cunningham once again shaking with laughter. Max was still scrubbing and his whole body was now as red as a beet. "Max. Looks like you boys just plain ran up against the wrong woman".

Ten

The trip back to Indianapolis took a little over two hours. Nancy had climbed up and sat next to Elk. It was then he told her of Oliver's death, and how Marshal Cunningham had taken him back to town. "Mother. We didn't know where this was going and I had Jack tell the undertaker to take dad to the Grant Street Cemetery. The main thing was to get you safe and I did the best I could. Looks like it didn't work out to well".

She nodded her understanding. "I knew about Oliver's gambling Richard. This whole mess is because of that. What's happened has happened because of that. I loved him, but there isn't anything I can do now about his death except see to it those responsible are brought to justice. I will grieve later. Right now we have other things to do". As he drove, she slept resting her head on his shoulder. She had slipped her arm through his arm and her hands were clasp together. Talk was quiet so she could get some much deserved rest.

Cunningham was on Elks horse, and pulled in close so they could talk without disturbing her. "R.E. You know that bunch McFarland worked for is most likely on their way to pay a visit to your father, don't you?

"I been thinking on that very thing. My father is going to need me".

Cunningham nodded in agreement. "I figure they have a day's head start on you. We can send a wire, but this is the kind of thing that needs to be handled by the law. There is bound to be some killing and like as not some innocent folks are going to be in the way. This trash smells gold and things will most likely get mean.

"When we get back to town I'd be obliged if you would take mother on to Crawfordsville in the morning. We can stay at Rena's place tonight and get the ball rolling early.

That bunch will be out of Chicago and even if they get to Cheyenne ahead of me, they will have to outfit to travel across country".

The Marshal looked into his young friend's eyes and reached over and took hold of the harness of the horse nearest him, and pulled the team to a stop. "Elk let me tell you something. I know you got this thing to do, but you and me go back a ways and there ain't any way in the world you're going to go up against these people by yourself. I have two damn good deputies that can look after things until I get back and so you can just count me in. I'm goin along. There ain't no reason your Ma there can't drive herself home. It'll take less than a day through some mighty pretty country. Hell she will enjoy it".

When Cunningham had pulled the wagon up, the lack of movement had awakened Nancy and she sat quietly listening to the other two. "All I have to say is when you buy tickets to Cheyenne, you better get three. I'll be going along".

Elk smiled and patted her hand. "Mother. You've done a lot of things you can be proud of. You made that long journey to Oregon with Peter. You took all those folks up north all during the war and risk your life several times, and you can be proud of that. But that was several years ago, and uh, you".

"And uh. I was what young man! If you are going to say I was younger, just speak right up and say it. Look at Jack there. Do you know we are the same age? Do you think for one minute he is ready for the bone yard? I little gray around the edges? Yes. A little more weight than he used to carry? Yes. A little slower than he used to be? Yes. Can he still get the job done? You bet he can, and so can I. I'm going and that's the end of it. Now get this wagon going, we're wasting time".

Elk grinned and started the team for town once again. He

looked over at Cunningham who was right now, not in the best of moods. "Damn glad you folks waited till I was out of hearing range before you run me down like that. A good thing I ain't sensitive. Body could get his feelings hurt, but what the hell, we're all friends here. Right, Nancy"?

She looked at Elk, who was grinning and gave him a loving elbow in the side. "Sorry Jack. I guess I shot my mouth off. I was just making a point".

"Uh huh. Well you made it, and yes you did. Elk you better pick up the tickets. Ain't sure I can make it over to union station and back. Spect' it's almost a mile round trip".

Eleven

It was late when they got to Rena's place. Cunningham tied Elks horse to the back of the wagon and headed for livery, a bite to eat, and a soft bed. "See you two in the mornin. Sleep well".

Rena herself greeted elk and Nancy at the door. "Please come in Mrs. Weliever. I know you are very tired. Your room is ready and I have had Mr. Franklin draw you a nice hot bath. Perhaps we can talk in the morning".

Nancy gave the beautiful young lady a hug and thanked her. "Rena, you are as beautiful as your mother. I hope she is well"?

"She is very well, thank you. She lives with my sister over on Blake Street. We are together every Sunday. She will be glad to know you are safe. Come. We must get you cleaned up so you can rest".

Elk watched the two women walk up the stairs and gave a sigh. In his own room he found Mr. Franklin had drawn him a bath as well. He undressed, climbed into the hot water and sank down as far as he could letting the heat soak out the stress of the day. When he was through, he dried off and sank into bed. He fell asleep thinking of tomorrow, and his people at the hands of the gang from Chicago.

It was sometime in the early morning he heard the bedroom door quietly shut and saw the shadow of someone moving toward the bed. The fragrance of Rena's perfume told him who was there even before she spoke. "Am I disturbing you, Elk"?

The soft moonlight coming through the window seemed to silhouette her against the darkness and made her even more stunningly beautiful than she already was.

Elk tried to speak but the air caught in his throat. The "No of course not". Came out as more of a croak than a statement. He watched in enchanted wonder as she untied her robe and let it fall to the floor. Without saying a word she reached over, pulled the bed cover back and slipped in beside him.

He raised up on one elbow and lay looking at her. So taken was he by her beauty, he could feel his heart beating in his throat. The creaminess of her skin and the magnificent sculpture of her body were like looking at a rare work of art. Reaching over, he slowly ran the tips of his fingers down her belly to the soft blackness that covered her womanhood. Gently, he began massaging the tip of one breast with his tongue.

This time, it was the air that caught in her throat. She took his head in her hands and moved to his mouth. Kissing gently at first then harder and harder until their tongues began to touch and explore one another. What followed was fleeting time of tender passion and adoration.

It was in the darkness just before dawn when he was awakened by the door to his room closing once again. As he drifted back into sleep, he realized he had been with the most beautiful woman he had ever seen. A sweet memory that he would call back time and again.

Cunningham came early for breakfast, and after egg's sausage and hot fresh bread the three of them said their goodbyes and headed for Union Station. Cunningham sniffed the air and then sniffed Elk. "My, don't you smell sweet this morning my young friend? What did you put in your bath? I may have to guard you when we get on the train. Some of those roughnecks may just take a liking to you. What do you think Nancy? Smells sweet, don't he"?

Elk looked at his mother to find her smiling. She covered her mouth and made a small cough. "Rena is very beautiful, don't you think Richard"?

"Hadn't thought much about it. I suppose she is at that". He wondered if the red around his neck had reached is face.

Cunningham looked at Nancy and reached over and felt

Elks face. "Damn R.E. you look a little flushed. You feeling all right"?

"Just a slight headache. Didn't sleep to well".

"Uh huh".

"Can we drop this? We got more important things to do than talk about how I feel. I'll be fine. Let's get to the train".

"Good idea. By the way, I'm fine. How about you Nancy? Are you fine"?

"Yep. I'm fine too. You do look fine Jack. Looks like we're all fine. Isn't that nice Richard? We are all fine".

"For crying out loud"!

For those listening. The two people laughing on the corner of Washington and West streets that morning could be heard for half a block.

Twelve

Union Station was busy this morning as it was every morning. Cunningham had already purchased the tickets for coach. This would allow them to watch the rest of the passengers without looking too suspicious. Their car was the third one back from the big steamer, and they wasted no time heading for it. About half way there Elk got the Marshals attention and then nodded his head in the direction of the baggage car. He heard the air whistle through the big man's teeth and saw his jaw tighten. "I count twelve, RE, how about it"?

"Twelve is right, Jack. Who are they? Or maybe I should ask where they from"?

"Only know one of them for sure. That short fat man doin all the talkin' is one of the big shots from a gang in Chicago. Only know him as Irish Bob. Ruthless bastard. If he's here, it's important to the higher ups. Never seen him in action, but I have heard he will sacrifice every man he has to get the job done. We got us a pack of trouble son".

Elk's first thought was of his mother. He turned toward her and started to speak. "Don't even think it, Richard. You're going to need me before this is over. Besides, I have an old friend to visit".

He nodded and turned his attention back to the baggage car. "Seems like a lot of baggage for no more than twelve men wouldn't you say, Jack"?

"Yep, and I'll bet my last dollar there is a whole lot more than clothes in them bags. Look how they are straining to get them in the door. Porter there ain't even allowed near em', most likely be a man in the car for the entire trip".

Elk started to respond, but just then the fat man turned and looked directly at them and waved. "Well, he sure as hell ain't scared of us. That's for sure. Think he knows who we are"?

"Not a doubt in my mind son. We best go ahead and get settled in. I have a feeling this is going to be a real interesting trip. I do intend to pay a visit to that baggage car before long though. Never can tell what we might find in there".

Once they were settled in, Elk decided to have a look around. "Might just as well test the water, I reckon. Thing that bothers me though, is this. There just isn't any way twelve men are going to take anything from those mountains. I don't care how many guns they have. There just aren't enough of them. To get what they are after they will have to have pack animals and someone to take them to the area. You can tell by lookin' at them they ain't never been outside the city, let alone go into the mountains in search of lost gold. Somethin' ain't right here Jack. There has to be more to it than this".

Nancy had been listening to both sides for quite some time. "Elk, Zac Farley told me one time how wolves hunt. There may be a pack here and a pack there, but in the end they all hunt the same. Those twelve city slickers we were watchin' are at some time or another going to meet up with more of their kind. I have a feeling that when that happens there is going to be a war. No one but those fightin' it may know, but it is bound to happen. That gold has been coming to me for years, and they know it. Blood is going to run and innocent people are going to die unless we get it stopped somehow. To be honest, I think we need to carry the fight to them starting now. Run them off and it will be over before it starts".

Cunningham laughed. "Damn Nancy, we can't just go around killin' folks, even if they are crooks. That's murder and you know it. As hard as this is going to get we got to play out our hand. Besides, gun play on a train is bound to get folks hurt that ain't got nothin' to do with this. Slow and easy is the way it's going to have to be. Don't seem right, but that's the way if it".

Elk patted his mother's hand and saying he would be back in a while headed for the front of the car. Once on the platform he swung around the side of the car, climbed the ladder and eased himself on top. Noting where his shadow fell, he crouched and softly padded forward to the baggage car, slipped back down the ladder and carefully opened the door. He had been right, there was a man posted here. Just now he had the sliding door open and was leaning back against the opposite wall smoking a cigarette. This told him most of what he needed to know about their baggage.

Acting as if nothing in particular was on his mind he shut the door and called a greeting to the man on the chair. "Hello there, mister, kind of lonely in here by yourself ain't it"? The sound of Elks voice startled the man. Slamming his chair down, he jumped up facing the young marshal with his hand inside his coat resting on his gun.

The badge pinned to Elk's vest did nothing to ease the man's fears. "Oh, hello there marshal. You startled me sneakin' in here like that. You come in the wrong way. All the passenger cars are behind us. How was it you did that anyway"?

Elk could see the man was nervous and decided to push a little. "Not much to it really, mister. I just walked across the top of the car, came down the ladder and opened the door. Didn't mean to scare you. Glad you're here though. I need to check those bags stacked right over there beside your chair".

The man looked at the bags then back at Elk. "I'm sorry, marshal, but those bags belong to my boss, and he don't want nobody messin' with them. Can't let you do that".

Elk grinned. "Well now, that does pose a problem. You see, I am a Federal Marshal and the law says if I want to look in those bags there I can sure do it. So why don't we quit this talking and just open them. I can take my look and be on my way".

The man's eyes narrowed just a bit, and his arm moved ever so slightly inside his jacket. The young marshal's movement was swift and sure. Sidestepping the man, he placed one hand on his wrist keeping him from pulling his pistol. With the other, he took a firm hold of his coat and in one swift motion threw him out the side door of the car. As it happened the train was passing over the Wabash River. Elk watched with interest as the man sailed through the air, fell fifty feet, and landed in the water below. Incredibly, the man surfaced and looked back at the young marshal. He saw Elk wave and disappear into the car.

A quick check of the bags confirmed his suspicions of the extra firearms. He spent the next five minutes throwing the gang's baggage into the watery ditch alongside the tracks. Closing the sliding door, he left the car the same way he had gotten in and returned to his own car.

Cunningham nodded a greeting. "You been gone most a half hour son. Thought I might need to come and get you. Everything alright"?

"Yep, the count is now down to eleven. Those eleven are going to be wearing the same underwear for the rest of the trip, or buy new in Chicago before we switch trains. They are now short on baggage".

Cunningham grinned. "You didn't. Nancy, you have raised a devil here".

"Don't blame me. He gets that rough stuff from his father. You know how I am. The soul of gentleness".

Elk shook his head and pulled his hat down over his eyes. "I need a nap. Wake me up when we get to Chicago".

The rest of the trip to Chicago proved to be uneventful and the change of trains made without incident. Nancy picked up some hot coffee and sandwiches from the station restaurant and a small bag of cookies. Tasting one, she thought of her own kitchen and smiled. Thought again of her broken table leg and became angry all over again. This was serious business and she aimed to keep her mind focused on the problem at hand. Blowing steam, the big locomotive spun its wheels a couple of times and pulled out of the station heading southwest. Carrying among other things a gang of well dressed thugs from both Indianapolis and Chicago all of whom were hell bent on stealing Indian gold whatever the price. Just two cars separated them from the three people who had set out after them to right the wrong of Oliver's death and prevent the death of even more innocents now in Wyoming. Murder had already been committed and there would be more blood spilled, much more, before this nasty business was finished.

Thirteen

Marshal Cunningham sat looking out the window in thought. Reaching inside his coat pocket he pulled out a small silver flask and started to put it to his lips. Pausing he offered it to the other two. "Nancy. Would you like a sip of this? Might take the edge off a bad situation here. Lord knows we are surly in a mess. Traveling with a gang of cutthroats not two cars back, I'll tell you the truth. It's hard bein' a lawman at times. I would like to just walk back there and start throwin' lead everywhere" Without waiting for her answer the big man put the flask to his lips then slid it back inside his pocket.

Elk had been sitting with his hat pulled down over his eyes listening. He watched as his longtime friend took a second then third pull on the whisky flask. Sitting upright Elk held out his hand for the flask. "Give it to me Jack".

Cunningham smiled and stood up. "Sorry pard, but it's empty. I'll go on back to the dining car and get it refilled. Be back in a minute".

Elk caught him by the coattail and stopped him. "Sit back down Jack. That won't be necessary. I don't want a drink, and you don't need any more either".

Cunningham was insulted. "RE. Just who the hell do you think you're talkin' to here? If I want a drink I'm damn sure going to take it and neither you nor anyone else has any say in it. Did you hear that Nancy? Mind your own business RE. And wipe that grin off your face. This ain't no laughing matter".

Elk tried without success to keep from smiling at his friend's tirade, but could not. The more he tried the funnier it got until both he and Nancy were both laughing.

Cunningham couldn't stand it anymore and jumped to his feet. This time it was Nancy who stopped him. "Please Jack. We are sorry. It's just that you get so worked up.

Please, sit back down".

Straightening himself up a bit the marshal took his seat once more and sat staring angrily at Elk. "Well, deputy. I'm waiting. And this better be good or I'm liable to fire you right here and now".

"Uh huh. Look Jack, it's like this. I have known you about all of my life and if we were out somewhere with that horn of yours it wouldn't matter to me if we got so drunk we had to sleep on the ground naked. But we have fourteen or fifteen men a couple of cars back that we are going to have to handle before this thing is cleared up. We need you sober Jack. You know damn well that you are about ready to walk back there and start gunplay. As much as it bothers me, those folks haven't broken the law as yet. So, that puts you on the wrong side of the law. Badge or not".

Cunningham's face had softened a bit and he rubbed his chin in thought. "Reckon you are right at that deputy. Fact is I was gettin' ready to settle this all by myself. Don't know as I could take the whole bunch of em' alone. You still want the flask"?

This time Elk did laugh. "What for? It's empty now, you big jerk. We do need to talk about those fine upstanding men though. Where do these people come from anyway? I mean they have some kind of boss back there that's dressed like he was a king or something. Wearing a white suit and a gray cape of some kind. What kind of a crook is that? How dangerous could a man like that be anyway"?

"He is the most dangerous of them all RE. As to where do they come from? Well, I've thought about that a bit and to me it's like a bunch of flies gatherin' around a dung heap. Same thing exactly for my money. Here's the thing though. A bunch like this starts out simple. You know, the kind of crooks that we deal with mostly. Only they begin to pool their money and the first thing you know they hire a couple of people who are educated to keep their books and deal out their money. They begin to buy legitimate businesses and are able to hide most of their dealings. A friend of mine calls it laundering' schemes. That way they are still able to do their regular stealing and blackmail and other things and not get caught most of the time. Where they mess up, at least this time is when there is a big score. Then they show their true colors. In each one of them, there is more greed than honor. They will kill each other over any amount of money. In this case, there is a great deal of money at stake. Moreover, even though they haven't seen it yet, just the thought of all that gold is enough to get the ball rollin'. As for Mr., fancy pants back there. He will have his goons kill you or he will be more than happy to handle it himself. So, the advice is to be careful".

Elk sat fascinated by his friend's knowledge and experience. Most of what he knew of the law he had learned from this man and just now he was very glad the marshal was along.

"Tell you another thing about people these folks. Many of them can't read or write. Still, a lot of them are among the smartest men I have come across. It seems that it is just much easier to start out stealing than to learn to read on the other hand those that are smart have some of the dumbest ones working for them. They do that because a stupid man is easy to please. A little money, or a woman on occasion, and a bottle of whisky will most of the time keep them loyal. There is never a shortage of men, or women for that matter, who are looking for easy money. And, I have seen some of those women who were a whole lot more dangerous than any man. Nancy, that woman that chased you all the way to Minnesota that time you and dog were taking that family north. That woman was mean clear through". [*Weliever's Railroad.*]

Nancy nodded and reached for her ten gauge. Thought better of it and left it resting where it was. She had learned long ago how intimidating this big double barrel was and the need to handle it not only with care but with consideration of those present. "We have other business now Jack. This bunch is out to hurt folks that I care about and I don't intend on letting that happen. I'll be very glad to see Elks father again. It has been a long time. Too long for that matter, he has been on my mind a lot of late". Elk smiled at her. "The feeling is still there isn't it mother. I for one am very glad of that. Father worships you. But, I think you have always known that".

Returning his smile, she said nothing, but her mind was racing back to that wonderful night at the hot spring. Her heart beat a little faster at the thought of their lovemaking. The sound of a strange voice brought her back to the present with startling suddenness.

Standing by Marshal Cunningham's seat, stood the leader of the bunch that they knew were after the Indian gold. A white suit, black walking stick made of a beautiful highly polished wood topped by a very large gold nugget and gray cape draped over his shoulders, secured at the collar by a large, and highly polished silver button. His arrogance was almost more than she could stand. This time when she reached for her ten gauge her intent was to make the man nervous. He didn't bat an eye.

Tipping his hat and bowing slightly, he introduced himself. "Good evening madam, marshal, I am very sorry to interrupt you, but I do have a matter of some importance to discuss. Looking at Elk and then at Nancy he continued. Madam, if you would tell your Indian servant to remove himself perhaps I can sit down and explain what I mean". Taking a step back and waited for Nancy to tell Elk to move.

Her response was instantaneous. In one swift motion she began swinging the big double barrel up and pulling both hammers back at the same time. Had it not been for Elks quick thinking the man would have had his body parts spread over most of the other side of the car. As it was, it was necessary for Elk to put the side of his hand between the hammers and firing pins to keep that from happening. Taking the shotgun from his mothers hand he too bowed slightly and with a cheery smile on his face got up, stepped past the grinning Marshal and out into the isle, allowing the man to sit directly across from his glaring mother.

"Thank you madam, but I must tell you your servant does need a lesson in manners. I have seen these savages before and have found there is but one thing they really understand. A good whipping will most often do the trick. If you wish I could have one of my men handle that for you. One or perhaps two whippings should do the trick. Then again, some of these savages never learn".

Marshal Cunningham, while amused at what had just happened had already grown tired of the conversation. He didn't like this man to begin with and what had just transpired made him more than a little angry. Besides, he wanted to see if the man really had the backbone he was rumored to have. Pulling his Dragoon, he pulled the hammer back and stuck it in the fat man's face. "Irish, I know who you are by reputation. We all do, even this Indian servant here. Suppose you tell us what it is you want and then get your ass out of that seat and be on your way. We were having a pleasant conversation here before you interrupted us".

Once again, the man didn't flinch, not so much as a twitch. The only thing the marshal could see were the pupils of his eyes narrowed a bit. Elk saw this as well and made a mental note of it. Knowing, that in a dangerous situation, this could be the little bit of edge that would mean the difference between life, and death.

Smiling, the big Irishman waited for the marshal to holster his pistol, then relaxed and leaned back in his seat.

"Actually, my name isn't Irish Bob as they call me. My real name is Keith Tully. I believe the name Irish Bob came from this unusual watch bob that I have worn for years. Pulling the bob from his vest pocked he revealed a small skull with a gold pin stuck through the opening where the ear should be. He saw Nancy shiver and smiled again putting the bob back into his pocked he continued. It seems that one of my men has disappeared. I started out with twelve and now I am down to eleven. Normally, that wouldn't bother me except this man was placed in the baggage car to watch over our luggage. He is now gone and our luggage as well. Very strange don't you think"?

Marshal Cunningham sat looking at the man in amazement. "Keith, let me see if I understand this. You of course know I am a United States Marshal. Is that right"?

"Yes it is".

Marshal Cunningham nodded and continued. "Well, Keith. Then you also know that I just plain don't have time to worry about your luggage. Now the disappearance of your man is another story altogether. What do you think happened to him"?

"I have no idea. The last I saw of him was when I assigned him to the baggage car. He had loaded our luggage and the door to the car was closed. The rest of us boarded the train and that is the last I saw of him. About an hour ago I sent one of the other men forward to relieve him so he could get his supper and that's when I got the news he was gone. Along with some very expensive clothing I might add".

The marshal rubbed his chin pretending to be in deep thought. "Uh huh. So as I see it you are down to the clothes on your back is that right"? Nancy began to smile. She had known Jack Cunningham for a very long time and she thought she knew what was coming. "I mean here you are headed west and your luggage has disappeared along with your man of course"?

"Yes, that's right".

"I see. Well then Keith, I guess the question I have now is just what the hell are you going to do for underwear for the rest of the trip. I mean, as big as you are, you are going to get to smellin' pretty damn ripe in a day or two. As I see it, you're in a bad fix man". Keeping the poker face he was known for, he looked at Nancy. "What do you think Nancy"?

The big Irishman could see her laughing at him and became angry. Getting up, he stepped out into the isle. "I see my troubles are going to be my own to solve. Don't underestimate me marshal. I didn't get where I am by being stupid".

"No, I just bet you didn't. But then, I bet you had clean drawers back then".

Watching the man storm back toward his own car Cunningham looked at Elk. "Okay you savage servant sit back down there and keep quiet".

Fourteen

Night came and went, but there was little sleep among the three. Irish Bob made no secret of the fact that he thought he was in control and that included the three of them. Morning sun found the three with red eyes and short tempers. Nancy couldn't even use the ladies room without being watched. She for one was out of patience with this cat and mouse game and was determined to bring it to a head one way or the other. Getting up she carefully folded her blanket and laid it in her seat. Reaching over she picked up her ten gauge and without a word started down the aisle toward Irish Bobs car. The mood she was in now it didn't matter to her if there were fifty of those scoundrels waiting. "We'll just roll the ball and see where it goes from there". She thought to herself as she approached the door to the next car.

As it happened the butt of her shotgun brushed Marshal Cunningham's leg as she moved carefully by him. He opened his eyes in time to see her approach the door at the other end of the car. Instantly he smacked Elk on the knee and motioned for him to look. "This is bad Jack". He said leaping up and starting out after his mother. "You ain't tellin' me a thing R.E. look at the way she is holdin' that scatter gun. Folks is going to start dying'. Hurry up! We got to get her stopped before it's too late".

Nancy was through the door and half way through the next car before the two reached the door. Swinging it open they rushed through in time to see her raise the ten gauge and swing around facing them. Before her sat eleven very nervous men and two more who were just now trying to think of where they might go to be safe if she decided to drop the hammers on the cannon she now held in her hands. Elk had heard this tone of voice before and he knew that she meant every word that she was now speaking. He and the marshal looked at each other and knew they were in a bad situation here. The only thing they could think of to do was squat down out of the line of fire. Both did so at about the same time. Reasoning that from here they could leap up and help if the need arose.

Elk peeked around the corner of the last seat in the car and could see that the eleven men were paying very close attention.

"Gentlemen, I am quite sure every one of you knows who I am. Just in case you do not, I am going to tell you. Before I do, however, I want you all to look very closely into the barrels of this ten gauge. I want you to do that because if you ever see these barrels again it will be the last thing you ever see. My name is Mrs. Nancy Weliever Stratton. I am on my way to Wyoming to visit some very dear friends of mine and to take care of some unfinished business. Now, I am quite sure you have been given instructions to watch me wherever I go. I really don't mind that you see until you start getting into my private time. Then I mind it very much. So I will tell you what we are going to do. You may continue to watch me, but when you see that I am going to the ladies room you run and tell the fat man in the dirty underwear that you can't watch me when I am in there because if you do I will shoot you. Is there anyone here who doesn't understand that? No? Good, then I expect no more trouble. Thank you gentlemen.

Setting the scattergun in the crook of her arm, she walked back up the isle toward her own car. As she passed the place Elk and Cunningham were hidden she stopped and looked at them. "You can come out of hiding now boys, mother took care of it". Both men stood up and followed her back through the door.

Marshal Cunningham was the first to speak. "Now ma'am, there just wasn't no call for you to talk to us like that in front of them boy's back there. What will they think? I mean we're Law Men".

"Who cares what they think Jack. Before this is over most of them, will be in a graveyard anyway, so why worry about it? At least they will if Irish Bob has his way. The man plans to make war on some people I care about very much and I aim to stop him. Turning, she looked at Elk. Do you have anything to say Richard? If you do keep it to yourself. I'm part of this and both of you will do well to remember it".

At two in the morning, Elk found himself unable to sleep. As much as he thought about the problem at hand, it was clear there was no easy answer as to how they were going to handle this situation. There was no doubt that his mother was right about others being involved in this scheme to steal the gold that had been a secret for so long. He hadn't seen them yet but knew they were coming. It was just a matter of time. "Who knows? They might be in place already. One thing was sure. If there were strangers about, the whole tribe would now it. They could try to hide or blend in but it wouldn't work. Not in this country, nothing moved in those mountains that someone didn't see. Strangers would stand out like snow on a mountaintop". Looking first at his friend Jack Cunningham then at his mother, he silently prayed he would be able to bring them through this mess in one piece. A man with friends was lucky indeed and he knew it was especially so with him. Growing up an Indian among whites had given him a look into both worlds and though his Indian world seemed a universe away right now, its peace overcame him and he drifted off with memories of those loving people around him.

Fifteen

Zacaria Farley and Peter Weliever had been making their way toward Running Elks summer camp for the last three days. Having just finished an eight year hunt for the killers of Peter's wife and child, they were at last coming home. Zac wasn't young anymore by any means. His old black skin had long ago been turned to leather by the life he had chosen. A hunter turned Indian scout, then family Zacaria had been over the mountain and across the creeks so many times it was believed he could find his way with his eyes closed at night. A blood brother too many of the Indians in this part of the country he was one of the very few that was respected.

Peter Weliever was Zac's son in law. He met the old hunter when he and his mother Nancy were moving west. Pete at sixteen had been a willing student in the art of living out of doors. Zac's daughter Fawn had been sixteen as well. Married by the Chief they moved on to Oregon, and with help built a very fine cabin and set up housekeeping. That had been almost twenty years ago. A daughter and a baby boy had been born during that time and life had been good. Pete and Zac had been out hunting one fall morning when a marauding gang of white trash came upon the homestead and raped then murdered Fawn and their daughter Nancy, named after Peter's mother. The gang cut off the baby boy's head and then set the cabin on fire. Zac saw the smoke first and the two of them rode hell bent for the cabin. They arrived to find the baby's head posted on a stick in the yard and the cabin in flames. It took two whole days shifting through the ashes to even find enough bones to bury. Pete dug the graves deep to keep their remains safe from animals. Then in silence the two of them mounted up and started out after the killers on a hunt that would ultimately last for eight years. [*The long Hunt*] They tracked the killers as far south as New Orleans and West as far as California. All but one begged for their lives, but their pleas fell on deaf ears. Throats were cut and heads rolled as both men administered vengeance and their own brand of personal justice. The hunt ended on a very hot afternoon in a mud hut in West Texas. Pete gutted the last man and left him for the flies. The ride home had been long and slow without much conversation. Each man knew he must now heal himself and get on about the business of living. Not an easy task considering the compromise each had made to their normal way of life.

Just now, both men sat their mounts looking down into the beloved valley where so long ago their happiness had begun. Memories flooded their minds of time that now seemed so long ago. Zac looked over at Pete with hollow eyes. "Son, I ain't right sure I can do this anymore. It's been a long and bloody trail we've followed and we just ain't the same anymore. Look at em' down there. Waitin' for us like we was somthin' special. We ain't Pete. Fact is I ain't so sure we ain't worse than them we hunted down and killed. I ain't rightly sure of nothin' anymore. Maybe we should just keep on ridin'".

Pete nodded his understanding. "You call it Zac. You say ride. We ride. Could go on to Montana I reckon".

Just then, an old friend stepped out of the shadows. "Little Bear, Peter Weliever, I thought this might happen. I have been where you now are. Your minds and hearts are very heavy with all things past. We have waited long for your return and now you are among us once again. We need to talk of many things". Running Elk took the reins of both ponies and led them down the hill and across the stream into camp. The people stood back respectfully letting the three of them through their ranks. A gentle touch here, a word there, was the only response from all of those who had known both men for so long. Arriving at Running Elk's lodge, he motioned for them to enter. Setting across from them, the old Chief looked for a long time into each man's eyes. "I see much pain even after all this time. My heart is heavy for you both. The women have made food and placed it in your lodges. Sleep and eat and then we will talk of many things. Welcome home old friends". The Chief rose and waited for the two men to leave the lodge then followed them out and stood silently watching as the women led them to their own lodges. Returning, he sat down and began to chant an ancient prayer of thanks for their safe return.

It was long into the morning when Peter Weliever stepped through the opening of his lodge and into the sunlight. "You slept late Pete. Haven't been up all that long myself. Coffee"? Pete walked over and sat down next to the old man. "Folks is leavin' us be for now. Reckon we got us some mendin' to do. I been sittin' here thinkin' about what we been doin' the last eight years son. Ain't sure it was right, but then somebody had to go after them boys and I reckon we was the ones to do it. I can learn to live with it. Let em' rot in hell".

"Guess maybe you're right about that. You know even after all of this time I see Fawns beautiful face every day. Not so much Nancy and Jason anymore, but Fawn, I see every day". Zac nodded and was quiet.

Running Elk sat watching the two for a while before he got up and walked over to the lodge. Pouring himself a cup of coffee, he sat down and began to tell them of the impending trouble. A short ways into the story Zac held up his hand and stopped the conversation. "Wait a minute Elk. You mean to tell me that you have this big stash of gold somewhere up there in them mountains and it has been there even long before your time? And, there ain't nobody knows where it is cept' you and Elk junior"?

"That is right Zacaria. The gold has been there since before my people came to this valley. My father showed me and his father showed him. This has gone on for a great many generations. The location had to be secret for many reasons. If the whereabouts of the gold had been known, there would have been no peace. It does seem now that the secret is no longer known only to a few, but perhaps now too many. Strange, how a small piece of a map hundreds of years old can bring so much trouble. What are your thoughts on this my friend"?

"Simple really Elk. The way I see it you have two choices. You can either give up this here valley and move, or you can fight. To fight means a lot of killin', and I for one don't want no more of that. You know as well as I do that if folks come after the gold and even one gets away it will start all over again. Either way, it's an ugly proposition. Sorry old friend, but there just ain't no easy answer for this one".

The disappointment showed on the Chiefs face. "I understand Zacaria. We are glad you have come home to us. We will handle this in our own way. Do not worry. Rest and get strong again. We will speak more of this later". In one fluid motion, the Chief rose to his feet and walked away.

Zac picked up a stick and began to poke around in the fire. "You know we can't walk away from this don't you Zac. These folks are family".

"Damn Pete. I sure trained you well. I'm surprised you ain't turned black by now. Married my daughter, moved me in with you and been ridin' together now for almost twenty years". "

Pete held his arm next to the old man's for comparison. He too was leathery and brown from many days in the sun. "Close, old friend but not quite. Don't make much difference though. I'm more like you than my own father. And, damn proud of it too. What say we go on over to that breakfast fire and get our day started right"?

The usual smack on the back came. "Now you're talkin' son. Now you're talkin. Then, we'll go over and have another talk with Runnin' Elk".

Sixteen

At the Chiefs suggestion the three packed enough supplies for three days and rode out of camp early the next morning. He had said nothing about where they were headed and neither Zac nor Pete had any idea. About midmorning Zac he reined his horse to a stop fixed himself a chew, and sat waiting for the Chief and Peter realize he had stopped. Running Elk had known Zac for almost fifty years and knew before he started back that there was going to be a serious powwow. The three of them sat there for a minute before Zac opened the conversation. "Where we goin' Elk? It ain't no secret that we ain't out here for no afternoon ride. If we are headed for the gold I ain't at all sure I need to see it to offer my help. So, let's have us a talk".

Running Elk nodded his understanding and decided to tell Zacaria the whole story. "We are about an hour from the place where the gold has been resting for longer than the people have been in these mountains. You must see it to understand what I am talking about Zacaria. I cannot ask you to risk your life for something you know nothing of. It is true we have been friends for these many years and I know I need not tell you anything, and still you will stand by my side in battle as you have many times before. This is different and you must see for yourself. Peter, you must see it as well, for you are one of us just as Zacaria is one of us. Be patient for a time longer, and then I will ask you to decide where you will stand".

Pete spoke up for the first time. "Chief, I know I married Zac's daughter, but I don't figure that makes me one of you. But I can say for sure that if Zac here says we will stand by you then that's the way it will be. No question about it".

Zac spat a stream of tobacco juice and nodded. "He's right Elk. We're with you, come hell or high water. But, you knew that all along didn't you"?

Smiling, the Chief turned his horse toward the North East and started out once again. Peter rode up beside the old man and was quiet for a while. "This is a hell of a big secret Zac. Do you think there is all that much gold"? "Don't know son, but if there ain't, there is sure a lot of fuss over nothin. I been all over this country around here for better than forty years and I ain't never come across no cave full of gold. Not right sure what I would have done with it if I had. I guess we'll just see directly. Here, want a chew"?

Pete took a small pinch and handed the bag back. "Ain't nothin like a good chew Zac".

The Chief had been right about the time. It wasn't more than an hour when he stopped and dismounted at the base of what appeared to be a shear wall running straight up for what looked to be a hundred feet or more. Zac sat his horse and watched him start up the side of the wall and then suddenly disappear. "Well, if that don't beat all! Did you see that Pete? Elk slipped into that crack in the wall there and was just gone. No wonder nobody has found that gold. There would be no reason to go up there. The wall is solid rock with only that little crack. C'mon son, let's have us a look see". When they started up the side of the rock wall both were surprised to find there were small hand and foot holds carefully cut into the rock. The climb was straight up, but it didn't take more than a minute or two of climbing for them to reach the place where Elk had disappeared. Stepping off into the crack they walked back into the center of the rock for a few feet. Elk was waiting for them holding a small torch. "Come Zacaria, it is but a short distance". The Chief started to turn, but Zac reached out and grabbed his arm stopping him. "Hold on Elk. Tell me about these drawings here. Zacaria stood with open mouth as the Chief moved the flame about. There before them were crude drawings that seemed to have been done with charcoal. Some were of ships at sea; some were of what appeared to be soldiers being killed by what had to be very early inhabitants of this part of the country. There seemed to be one drawing of a land mass and leading from it were charcoal marks across the sea to another land mass. Zac guessed this was where they were now. There were drawings of soldiers killing the natives and taking their gold away by pack animals. The writings he did not recognize, but the intent of this hidden place was plain. Whoever these people were, they had intended to return here one day. Otherwise there would have been no map. Elk, Pete, look at this. This happened a very long time ago. Hard tellin' how far these folks packed this stuff. It's been said that down in Mexico or thereabouts, there was an ancient civilization that had all kinds of gold. Made plates and jewelry out of it. Could be that is where this came from. Is there much of it Elk"?

"Come, and see for yourself. It's this way". The Chief moved deeper into the cave and every step revealed more drawings. "I always thought there were a great many of those who moved the gold. There is so much of it. It is here". Handing Zac the flame he walked to the back of the cave and began removing stones from a hole that had been cut into the wall. Peter moved to help and after some ten minutes they had exposed a small room of about ten feet by ten feet. The ceiling was not more than four feet high but in this space was stacked leather bag after leather bag of refined gold dust. It measured the full ten feet by ten feet and at least three feet high.

Peter stood staring at the pile and then slowly sank to his knees. "Zac, my mind won't come around this. What are we going to do? How can we possibly help"?

Zac seemed more interested in the leather pouches than the gold itself. "You see these bags Pete. They ain't a bit rotten. I mean they are dusty, but seem to be in perfect condition. Must be because they stayed dry from bein' walled up all this time. No moisture. Ain't that somethin' though? A lot of it too, this took a while to get in here. Had to be quite a few of these men to do this".

"Many of them are still here Zacaria". Holding up the torch the Chief walked a few steps to the other side of the cave. There, placed in a neat row were the bones of several men. "I believe these were the soldiers who were left here to guard the gold. Many years ago our people moved these bones here in respect. These men had to believe that others were coming back for them. Some tragedy must have happened and all died of starvation. You can see these shields of war and the long blades. Some had clubs with iron spikes driven deep into them. These men were violent warriors".

Zac rubbed his chin the way he always did when he was thinking hard. "Could be you're right Elk. One thing for sure though, this is one hell of a mess of gold. What do you plan to do with it? And, why in the world would anyone bring it clear up to Wyoming? Could be they were on the run and heading for the coast west of here. Might be they just plain got overrun and put the stash here intendin' to come back for it"

"That is what we must talk about Zacaria. It seems we are not the only ones who know about it. As I have told you after all of these years a map of its location has appeared. I am afraid I am to blame for the trouble that is coming to our people. Peter, this involves your mother Nancy and even your brother Richard. My heart is very heavy over this and we have much talking to do. I show you this because you must understand the danger that is coming to us".

"Peter was quiet for a time then seemed to get mad. "Well, it ain't like we haven't had trouble before. Like mother always says, let's take it to em' and get it over with. What's

comin' anyway"?
"Whatever it is this ain't the place to talk about it. Elk,
what say we head on back to camp and do this talkin' over
a good meal and a warm fire? I for one could use a roof
over my head and a nice soft bed, for a change. We can
come back here anytime. I got a couple of ideas about this
anyway".
"Elk smiled at his old friend. "Zacaria, if this was a few
years ago you would have been thinking of something else
to go with that soft bed. He slapped the old man on the
back and in spite of the trouble all three laughed".
"Uh huh. Tell you somethin' old friend. That ain't nothin
anymore but a pleasant memory".
Again the Chief smiled. "I don't believe you for a minute
Zacaria Farley. I have known you for too long".
The climb back down the face of the wall posed no
problem. Zac stopped about two hundred yards from the
wall and looked back. "You just plain can't tell anything is
there. Beats all I ever seen. Pete, we got us some serious
thinkin' to do about all this".

Seventeen

The late eighteen hundreds were exciting times in America. Many new things were being brought to the marketplace and yet the west was still young, wild, and dangerous. Railroads were stretching out across the country. From New York State, West to Montana and on to the Golden State of California, then South to Texas, rails were either being put down or there were plans to put them down. A newfangled contraption called the "horseless carriage" was being seen now and again on the city streets. These smelly "automobiles" as they would eventually be called were destined to take over the entire world. Even the friendly bicycle was to be "motorized" in America by a couple of brothers by the name of Davidson. William, Walter, and Harley Davidson. A name that would stand strong for America through many trials including war and depression, a name that would proudly bare the symbol of this great country to every corner of the world. Tremendous opportunity would bring peoples from all nations to America. Many came seeking freedom to live as they saw fit. Many more came to work the backbreaking jobs on the rail lines and in the gold and silver mines of the West and North.

A great many fine people migrated to America during those exciting years of growth and expansion. Unfortunately, not all of those who came to her shores were as upstanding as most. On the other hand, America it seems either brought out the best or the worst in people. Some would say it was the freedom that everyone had here that did it. In the old countries the law was so strict that anyone caught breaking it was so severely punished that to do so was deliberate and any punishment was warranted. In America however there was so much freedom and the country was so large that it was not only difficult to know who was breaking the law, but also where they were once the law found out who, they were.

Just like today it mattered not whether one was rich or poor. Opportunity to make easy and quick money appealed to all those who were willing to commit violence and take the necessary risk needed to live the life of crime. Just now there were eleven of those who had done so one car back from Nancy, Jack, and Richard running Elk.

The train pulled into Cheyenne about three in the morning. It had rained and the street lamps now sat in a shadowy mist. Leaving the platform the three stepped off into the muddy street and walked across the hundred yards or so the livery. Elk stepped to one side and off into the shadows while Jack and Nancy went on inside to arrange for horses to ride for the remaining sixty miles or so to Running Elks Camp.

Marshal Cunningham walked to the back of the shop and knocked on the door to the tack room waking the stable hand from a sound sleep. Standing at the door the marshal listened to the man grumble for a few minutes before opening the door. It was plain the man wasn't used to being awakened at this time of morning and his mood showed it. He started to say something then noticed the badge pinned to the Marshals vest and thought better of it and stepped out closing the door behind him. "Whatcha' want this time of mornin' Marshal? Ain't nobody here but me? Matter of fact it's been kind of slow, as of late".

Jack looked the man over and was surprised at what he saw. This had to be the cleanest liveryman he had ever seen. Looking around he knew why. The entire livery was clean. The harness had been separated and hung together, saddles and blankets all on stands or hung over stall rails; even the floors of the stalls were clean. "Mr., this is the cleanest livery I've ever seen. Don't you have no business at all"?

The man smiled and looked up as Elk came through the door and walked over and stood beside his mother. They had lit a lantern and were just now looking over the stock in the stall. "Well, to tell you the truth Marshal, I like to say we don't have much business but as a matter of fact we do. At least now, and today was a really big day. Rented almost all of everything I had. Could have rented that stock them folks seem so interested in but they ain't out stock. Injuns brought em' in here a couple of days ago and paid me in gold to hold em' for some folks comin' in on the train. Reckon you couldn't be them, could you"?

"Could be, but suppose you tell me about your day today".

"Well, actually it weren't today. It was yesterday. This bunch came in here and rented just about everything I had. Horses, wagons, even a carriage. Headed up North somewhere I reckon. Least ways that's what it looked like to me. Rough bunch out of Texas, or so they said. Paid the askin' price and said they would be gone for two weeks or better.

Elk had taken an interest in the conversation. 'You mean they took everything you had"?

"Yep, that's the reason the place is so clean right now. I was able to get up this mornin' and get her done. I usually keep on top of things anyway, but today was a might easier with the stock gone. Ain't no charge for you folks on them Injun ponies. Already paid for. That is if you are the ones they are meant for".

The young Marshal nodded. "We're the ones alright. The folks that brought them in were Shoshone and likely paid in gold. I expect they told you they were for Richard Running Elk. Is that right"?

"Right as rain young fella. You just go right ahead and take them. It will be daylight before long and you folks can get some breakfast over at Dorothy's and Emma's place in about twenty minutes. Matter of fact I aim to go over there myself this mornin' can't stand but just so much of my own cookin'".

For the next half hour or so Elk questioned the man about the gang that had taken his stock. He couldn't blame him for renting to them because it wasn't every day in this part of the country that a businessman was offered that kind of money. He learned that there were at least fifteen of them and most likely the man was right about them being out of Texas. That meant the gang on the train had contacted them in advance of their departure from Chicago and knew exactly where they were going to meet when they arrived in this area. Jack Cunningham guessed that when the mountains had slowed the train, the gang had slipped off and joined up with the others. That would have put them off the train several hours ahead. They also learned that the gang had bought many items from the local mercantile. This apparently was meant for an extended stay in the mountains if need be. Marshal Cunningham didn't like the way this was shaping up. "RE., Nancy, we got us a hell of a mess here. These murdering bastards are hours ahead of us and most likely will be lying in wait for us on the trail ahead. There are three of us, and who knows how many of them"?

Nancy got mad. Something she didn't do often, but she had had enough of these people. "I want to know just who these people think they are! Those are my friends up there in those mountains and nobody is going to go up there and hurt them in any way if I have any say in it. It seems to me like I have been fighting trash like this all my life. It's time we take the pain to them. I've lost my husband. I've been kidnapped, and I've been beaten. Boy's, I've had enough, let's get some breakfast and as Zac always said, "Get the ball rollin'".

The look on her face left no mistake about the stakes of this game. Stakes were high, with lives on the line they were as high as they were likely to get. The horses left them by Elks father and the other braves were exceptional. Food was there for the trail as well as ammunition, water, bedrolls, and skins to cover them against the weather. They picked up the trail almost immediately and followed at a gallop resting the horses as they walked every few miles. Indian ponies were famous for being able to go for hours on end, nevertheless, they had no way of knowing how long they would have to keep this up before they caught up with them so it was necessary to keep them as fresh as possible. It had rained a few days past but not enough to slow the wagons much.

Marshal Cunningham pulled up and dropped to the ground. Taking out a handkerchief he wiped the sweat off his brow and lit a store bought cigarette. Let the smoke drift through his nostrils and looked around. Nancy and Elk had been pushing hard for the last hour and it showed when they came back and pulled in beside him. "What's the matter Jack? Why are we stopped"?

The Marshal looked at both of them then back at Elk. "You know damn well why we're stopped RE. We are stopped because I want us all to get there in one peace. We have no idea in hell how many men are involved in this thing and to just ride blindly on is suicide. And you know it. You do too Nancy. I'm surprised at the both of you. Now let's take a few minutes here and get this thing organized".

He was right and they knew it. "Good idea Jack. Son, you gather up a little firewood we'll brew some coffee and start making plans to keep from being surprised by this scum. We do have to get ahead of them somehow though".

"That won't be a problem mother. I was raised in this country and nothing says we have to stick to the roads. It will be rough going in spots, but we can short cut them and pick up almost a whole day. If we press on through the night we should be ahead of them by morning".

The next hour or so was spent resting the horses and making plans to get ahead of the gangsters and even ways to stop some of them along the way. The plans weren't perfect, but at least now there was a plan in place. It was late afternoon when they left the road and started cross country to get ahead of the gang.

Eighteen

Elk pretty well knew the lay of the land. He had been raised further north but the Shoshone were hunters and from his earliest childhood he had accompanied his father as they rode far and wide in search of the necessary winter meat for the people. "Remember what you see here Elk. Remember how the land looks. There may be a time when you are alone or in trouble and will need what you learn here today. It often means the difference between life and death. So learn well son". Elk smiled as he thought of his father's teachings for those many years. The advice had been good for he had used the skills he had learned many times. Some had indeed saved his life. His mother speaking to him interrupted the young marshal's thoughts.

'You seem pretty far away son. Anything I should know about"?

"Just thinking of all the times Pop had told me to pay attention to where I was or what was around me. When you think about it the early people of this land had to be very wary of their surroundings all the time. As beautiful as it is here, there always seems to be danger around you. A bear will rise up out of nowhere, or an enemy will come over the hill. You never know when you're being watched".

"That's true enough, I guess. I remember years ago when Bill Allison was in a fight to the death with that she bear. Not too very far from here as I recall. If it hadn't been for Zac and the hound, he would have been killed. Your brother Pete and Uncle Feather had some part in that fracas as I recall. The hound was even in the thick of that one. I believe Bill still has that old bearskin put away somewhere. By the way does it bother your father when you call him Pop"?

He grinned at his mother. "He never says anything when I call him that, but I think it does bother him a little. You know how proper he is all the time. I think he allows it because I'm half white. Besides I do it to tease him. He will be very glad to see you mother".

She caught his meaning and kept her eyes straight ahead so as not to give away her excitement of returning after all these years. Thinking back to that time many years ago of that soft moonlit night and their passionate encounter at the hot springs made her heart race a bit. It was to her as if it had been only yesterday. She could still feel the power in his body, and hers as well as they became one on that special night. She had loved Oliver, but never had she had an experience that matched the passion and intensity of that night so long ago. Her skin grew hot and her throat tightened a bit. This was a memory she would have always and she was glad for it.

"Why mother, I believe you are blushing. Could it be that you are anxious to see father once again? He is still quite a man you know. A little older and wrinkled from the sun, but strong as ever".

Her eyes flashing anger she snapped at him. "Richard. You will not show me disrespect. I don't care how old you are. I'm still your mother and you will show me respect. Do you understand young man"? Not waiting for his answer she pulled up and then fell in line behind Jack. A little miffed at Elks importance, but also glad to hear that his father was in good health. The smile didn't show, but her heart was singing nonetheless.

Elk suddenly pulled up short and motioned for them to be still and dismount. "We got company he whispered. Couldn't be more than three hundred yards over that rise there. Must be setting up camp for the night. Scouting us out I reckon. If we're quiet we can get the jump on them and not be heard. On the other hand I don't want mother involved in any gun play".

The glare from his mother set him straight. There would be

no more of that kind of talk no matter how well meaning it was. They were all in this together and if they were going to make it to the town at all they would each have to do their part. He nodded his understanding to her and started up the rise to have a look. When he returned his face was grim with worry. "Saw four men and five horses. Hard tellin' where the other one is. Could be taking care of business or gathering firewood. In any case we can't wait around here for long. Either we handle this now or ride on. What do you think Jack? He had intentionally not asked his mother's opinion and she had caught it.

Marshal Cunningham started to speak but she held up her hand cutting him off. Moving within inches of Elks face she began to speak through clenched teeth. "Elk, I don't swear. You know that. We don't have time for this protecting me bullshit anymore. We are in this together and if I hear one more word out of you about this I will go on alone. Do you understand what I'm telling you son"? Nodding his head in embarrassment. "Yes ma'am won't happen again".

Cunningham's snicker brought her head around and the look in her eyes cut him off as well.

Elk continued, "As I see it we got two choices here. We can ride around and hope they will stay put long enough for us to get clear, or, we can face them down, here, and now. The thing is if we ride on, there is always that chance that they will pick up our trail and come upon us when we least expect it. My vote is to take care of this now. What do you think Jack"?

Cunningham rubbed his chin and looked at Nancy. She picked up the double barrel and stood waiting. The Marshal smiled and turned back to Elk. "The thing is, we can't just go rushing in there. If one of you was to get hit, I would feel real bad. Ain't no way we can surround them being backed up against that stone wall the way they are. So, what's the plan"?

Nancy spoke up. "We talk to them and tell them to leave".

Elk smiled, "What do you mean we talk to them"?

"Well, they don't know we're here and we will be above them. We spread out along the ridge there and just tell them to ride on. We will have the drop on them and if need be we can fire a few rounds to make our point".

The Marshal liked it and said so. "Damn good idea Elk. These boys are on some body's payroll and it most likely won't take much to get them moving. Especially if you mother fires that scattergun of hers. Down in that gully that thing will sound like a cannon. My bet is, we won't even have to kill anyone".

Elk nodded. "That's it then. You do the talkin' Jack. You sound like an old bear anyway".

The Marshal fainted hurt feelings. "I beg your pardon young man, and just who was it that did the playin' and singing at the dances on Saturday nights in town"?

"Sorry Jack, as drunk as you always got I'm surprised you remember them at all".

Nancy had had enough. She started up the hill, then stopped and turned around. "Can we just get on with this for crying out loud? You two are like a couple of kids".

Once on top, they spaced themselves about twenty feet apart. Marshal Cunningham checked the to be sure they were well hidden from below and then called out. "You men down there. This is U.S. Marshal Jack Cunningham. I want you men to mount up now and ride back the way you came. I'm going to be on your tail and if you stop before you get clear of this country here a bout, I will gun you down. Now get movin! You got one minute to get them horses saddled and out of my sight".

The answer came in the form of a bright flash fired from a heavy rifle higher up, and about thirty yards to the right. The heavy slug kicked dirt in Cunningham's face, missing him by inches and causing him to jump. Both barrels of Nancy's ten gauge fired an instant later, causing him to jump back the other way. There was a moan and then silence. Cunningham decided to press the issue. "That's one boy's. Do you want to continue this or move on"? After the camp moved out in the direction of their back trail, Elk went over to check on the bushwhacker that had fired the shot at Jack. He returned without saying anything until they were once again headed toward his summer camp. Cunningham sided in beside him. "Was the man hit bad? All I heard was the moan".

"There wasn't much left of him. I'm surprised he could even moan. My God, that is a terrible way to die, Jack. That boy was tore clear up. I can imagine how that woman from Georgia looked after the face off her and mother had that time in Minnesota. That is one terrible weapon, and she has carried it as long as I can remember. I think it belonged to her first husband, he must have been quite a man".

Nineteen

Zacaria, Pete, and the Chief were on their way back to camp when a pair of riders came into view. The Chief could see it was two men from the camp and if they were riding that hard it could, and most likely did, mean trouble. The men's horses were caked with sweat and stood quivering from fatigue from the run, but, like all Indian ponies would have continued to run until they died of exhaustion. Zac and Pete both spoke Shoshone and the message they were now hearing, did indeed mean trouble. They listened intently as the two men told of the fifty or so riders camped to the south about fifty miles. Well armed and rough looking men, they had been followed for the last week and it was believed they were heading straight for the camp. There were also a group of riders coming this way from Cheyenne. Also well armed, and they were being followed by Elk, a woman and what looked to be a US Marshal.

"My God, Chief that would be Nancy, and the Marshal is most likely Jack Cunningham. We better hightail it back to camp. There sure as hell seems to be a storm brewin', and that's for sure".

Pete took off his hat, wiped the sweat from his brow and sat looking toward the east. "Zac, you got any idea how long it has been since I last saw my mother? It's been almost twenty years Zac. My God, we didn't even wait for her to come out after those sorry bastards murdered Fawn and the children. We just started out after them. I haven't seen her since she left the valley and moved back to Indiana. I've become what I hated. Become what I killed. Maybe, I should just move on".

The Chief had motioned the two riders away and both he and Zacaria rode the few steps and pulled in beside Pete. Zac spoke first. "Son, me and you parded up when you were just a pup. I watched you grow into a man and a damn good one at that. You married my daughter and gave me grandchildren. This is the west son, and when those sonsabitches took all that we both loved, we, you and me, Pete, did the only thing we could do. It's true, you got some rough edges now. Hell fire son, we been on the killin' trail for eight long years. You can't shake a thing like that off overnight. It'll take some time, and that beautiful mother of yours will understand that".

The Chief swung his horse around and came in close facing Pete. Placing a strong hand on the young man's shoulder he looked him square in the eyes. "Peter Weliever, you are much respected among our people. You know that. For many years now you have been blood of our blood. You are one of us and I do not believe you will leave now that we need your courage. No, my son, you and your strong heart will be at our side, whatever comes. Even now, your brother rides to our side from the south. Together we will stand against this enemy whoever he is and together we will be victorious".

Pete's eyes had become downcast during all of this and when he raised his head and looked at the Chief once again, there were tears in them, for the first time in years. "Yeah, well, I guess maybe you two are right at that. Hell, ain't nothin' like a good gun battle to set things straight. Right Zac"?

Zac spat a nasty string of tobacco juice toward the south. "Right you are son. Bring the bastards on, we'll show em' fighting Indian style. Let's ride boys, we need to do some plannin' for this one. My God, I hate vultures like that".

Pete nodded, "You know, Zac. All of these men ain't comin' out here just to look at the scenery. They are after the gold and there has to be a reason for that after all these hundreds of years it has been sitting there. That most likely means a map of some kind. These folks bein' from the east and all, will likely have it with them. Seems to me that if we head them off and recover the map, all the rest of it will fall away and that will be the end of it. I mean hell, if them boys ain't going to get any money, they won't stay, and the whole bunch will head back the way they came".

For the first time in a very long time, fear rose up in the old hunter's chest. He knew where Pete was headed with this and he didn't like it. For the past eight years the only reason Pete had for being alive was to avenge the death of his family. That alone, was what had made him so dangerous. Time after time, Zac had seen the terror in the eyes of those they had tracked down. He had heard them plead for mercy, some on their knees. He had seen the stone cold hate in Pete's eyes as he gunned them down one by one, and left them lying where they fell. He had even killed one man while he was setting at his own dinner table with his wife and children. There was no mercy, just eight years of blood and death, and it had taken its toll. The young, and gentle farm boy who had come with his widowed mother to this far western land had changed. Peter Weliever was now like the country that now surrounded them. He was as dangerous as any she bear or mountain cat protecting her cubs. Over the years he had learned all the ways of the Indians he now called family. Only the color of his skin set him apart from those he loved so dearly. His blood was as their blood, he had come to hate his heritage, the white man.

"I know what you're thinkin' son, and it might work, but, you ain't goin' to do it. Now that the long hunt is over you ain't goin' to ride off somewhere and get yourself killed. Won't let you do it, so get the notion out of your head".

The look in Pete's eyes was suddenly distant and soft.

"Zac, you remember the first time we met.? You stepped out onto the trail and ask if we were circus folks"?

"Yep, I remember. Lord that was funny. Your mother

standing there whistling at them mules draggin' that wagon around and around in a circle like that. Beat anything I ever seen".

"That was over twenty years ago Zac, and I have been riding with you almost every day since that time. Now, if I decide to go off on my own and do something that's the way it is. My business, no one else's".

By the time Pete had finished, Zac was setting straight up in the saddle and there was fire in his eyes. "You think so huh. Let me tell you somethin' boy, you're about all I have left in this world and you start to do somethin' stupid like that and I will ride after you and drag you back here. If you think different, just try me. If you think for one minute I am going to try and explain to that mother of yours why I let you go and kill yourself you got another think comin'".

Pete laughed out loud. "She is a bit hard to talk to at times ain't she"?

This time it was the Chief who laughed. "Well, well, two real bad men of the west, afraid of an old woman. I can't wait to tell her".

"Oh, is that right? Well, Mr. Chief, you do that and Pete and me will tell her you said she was old. Besides, you ain't seen her in a spell. She may be just as beautiful as ever".

"Zacaria, you are indeed a hard man. Come, we have much to do. And, Pete does have an idea that we need to talk about".

Everyone in camp knew of the coming threat, and preparations were being made to not only defend the camp, but to take the fight to the enemy as well. There were a few older men that remembered the last time a bunch of killers had visited death on the camp. Those women and children who didn't have time to hide were slaughtered like buffalo on the plains.

Just now, the Chief, Pete, Zac, and seven or eight of the elders of the tribe were in the council lodge talking about the upcoming battle. They had been there about an hour when a small commotion outside the door diverted their attention. Pete pulled his pistol and started for the entrance when Elk and Jack Cunningham walked in. Elk embraced his father. "Sorry we are late, but we had a bit of trouble on the way in. Father, this is the man I work for, Captain Jack Cunningham, of the US Marshal Service. Jack, you pretty much know everyone else here".

Cunningham shook hands with the Chief. Then Zac and Pete. "Zac, it's been a while, and Pete, I understand you have been on a very long hunt. I've done a bit of that myself. Nasty business, takes a while to work that kind of thing out of your system". Turning back to the Chief, he continued. I don't come here to intrude my friend, but to help in any way I can".

The Chief gestured toward the circle of men still sitting. "You are welcome here Marshal. We are making talk about the trouble that is coming. We will listen to anything you have to say. Many years ago we had trouble much like this and we do not intend to let anything like that happen again. Please, sit down and join us".

Once seated, the Chief turned to his son. "Running Elk, tell me of your trouble on the trail. How many men are coming against us"?

A dark shadow came over Elk's face as he began to tell his father of the abduction of his mother, and the deception and finally the death of his step father. Each man's eye's reflected the pain and sorrow they felt for Nancy in this situation. "They're a dirty bunch, they murder anyone who gets in the way of what they want. And, what they want right now is gold that has been hidden for many years. It seems they have a map of some kind and are even now on their way here".

As Peter Weliever sat and listened to his brother explain the circumstances surrounding his, and Jack Cunningham's presence here. His mind drifted back to a happier time. He remembered taking lunch to his father each day as he worked the fields of their Indiana farm. Of his father teaching him to shoot, and of the neighbors, the Baker's coming over for Sunday dinner. He remembered the awful day Charlie Baker knocked on the door and delivered the message that his father had been killed coming home from town. Of saying goodbye to his father for the final time as he and his mother drove the wagon out of the yard heading west. There had been some happy times since then to be sure, but, there had also been almost unbearable pain in his heart many times.

Peter stood up, picking up his rifle, he turned to face the others, and when he began to speak the icy tone to his voice caused all in the room to be silent. "All we ever wanted was to live in peace and work our farm. To be part of this beautiful land and our friends, the Shoshone. Each time we tried, the greed of others came and hurt us, came here, to our homes and killed our children and our women. Burned our homes and destroyed our way of life. People who know nothing of our ways, come here to murder us, rape and kill our women and I for one have had enough of them. My love of the people rests strong in my heart and I understand you must make your plans, but for me. I will take my own vengeance on them. I will destroy them one at a time until I am either killed, or they are gone". When he had finished he turned and left the lodge without another word.

Elk started to rise and attempt to talk to Peter, but the hand of his father on his arm stopped him. "It is not your place to go to him my son. He loves you, and you him, but now it is in him to do what he must. His destiny is in the hands of those who ride the wind of the past. They will be with him until it is his time to join them. If he survives, he will be greater still, if not, he will be remembered by us always, until we join with him and ride the winds with our ancestors".

Zac rose and started out of the lodge, then turned, facing the Chief. "Take care of yourself old friend. See you on down the trail a ways, I reckon. Got to watch the boys back, or he, mine, ain't much difference anymore. We're about alike on that score". Nodding to the others he stepped out the door and followed Pete.

Cunningham let Zac clear the door of the lodge before speaking. "My God, RE, did you see the steel in them two boys. They have to be the hardest two men I have ever seen. Gives me the chills just to think of having them after me".

Elk, nodded his agreement. "Had a rough time, the both of them. That bunch camped south of here will have hell to pay, I'll tell you that. Pete just ain't anybody to mess with. Zac either for that matter".

"Uh huh, how old you reckon Zac is any"?

The Chief laughed, "Marshal, Zac never seems to age. Many years ago I asked him when he was born. He looked at me and said, "In the summertime".

Twenty

Zac no sooner stepped through the door when he spotted Pete talking to his mother. Not wanting to interfere, he started toward his own lodge, but stopped when he heard that familiar voice. "Zacaria Farley, you old grouch, don't you try and sneak away from me. I've come a long way to see you two".

He turned around just in time to brace himself against her hugs. Hugging her back, he held her at arm's length looking her up and down. "Lordy, Nancy, you ain't changed a bit. Just as beautiful as ever. Hear you had a bit of a run in with some bad folks comin' in".

Kissing him on the cheek she reached out and grabbed Pete pulling him to her and stood between the two of them with an arm around each man's neck. "Oh, it's so good to see you two here in camp. I'm glad you're back and finished with that business. You have been gone for so long. Peter, you should have written once in a while, I worried so much".

Pete was standing with hat in hand looking at her. "Truth is mother, me and Zac have been on the move pretty much for the past eight years. Wasn't a lot of time to write. Sorry for that, but that's the way of it. Fact is, we are on the way out right now. Got some business with these men that are comin'".

Nancy was shocked and it showed. "What! Why son you can't leave now. I have just gotten here. We have a lot to catch up on". Turning to Zac for support she said, "Zacaria, settle this boy down, will you? For heaven's sake, I need to spend some time with both of you".

Pete kissed her on the cheek and turned and walked away. She watched him go and then turned back to Zac. The old man looked at her and saw the tears of hurt in her eyes. "This ugly business has changed him Nancy, he ain't the same person anymore. Hell, neither am I for that matter. I'm mighty glad you're back where you belong. It's about time too". Patting her arm he headed after Pete.

"Take care of him Zac, bring him back to me".

"He takes care of me now Nancy, has for a long time. By the way, there's someone inside who will be mighty glad to see you".

Standing with a lump of sorrow in her throat, she watched as they mounted and rode out of camp leading their pack animals. Thinking to herself that Zacaria was right. Pete had changed. She only hoped his heart hadn't grown as cold and hard as his eyes. Stepping through the door of the lodge she was greeted by all as the old friend she was.

Taking a seat between Elk and the Marshal, she sat quietly listening as they began to make plans to defend the camp. Three times during the afternoon Elk noticed his father lean forward a bit looking around Elk at her. The third time the young Marshal chuckled and promptly caught an elbow in the ribs for his trouble.

Zac and Pete were about an hour out of town before either one said a word. The old man reined his horse in and sat still. Pete didn't notice at first and rode on for about fifty yards, then turned around, came back, and pulled in beside him. He sat looking at the old man without saying anything.

"You was kind of rough on your mother back there son. Weren't right neither, didn't like it much. I'll tell you that".

Pete took his hat off and setting it on the saddle horn wiped the sweat from his forehead on the sleeve of his shirt.

"What do you think I should have said? I haven't seen her in ten years, eight of which, I have spent hunting down, and killing people. You think I should have told her about all of that? We have blood on our hands Zac, and lots of it. I ain't at all sure it will ever wash off neither".

"We did what we had to do Pete. There weren't no other way to it, many times on that hunt I wanted to pack it in, but my daughter, and grandkids lay cold and dead at their hands. I was filled with hate, and wanted, not needed to make it right. Not for me, but for them. Hell, if that leaves blood on my hands, then I'll live with it. Now, how do you want to handle this business we're into now"?

Pete shrugged. "Ain't much to it. We know what these men are and why they're comin'. We been hunting this country for years and know it well, and they don't, so we stay above them and on the move. When we have the chance we empty as many saddles as we can and move again. I figure if we do that enough it will spook them bad, and give us the advantage".

"You mean bushwhack them. Is that it"?

"I don't care what it's called. I aim to run em' off".

"I like it, when do we get the ball rollin'"?

"Right now seems about right to me".

"You're mean boy. You know that"?

"Yep".

"Uh huh. Well then, let's ride".

Twenty one

As the last rider left the canyon Cunningham turned to the others. "Think they will ride on or turn back and try to hook up with their gang".

"Don't know, but after we check on the one mother returned fire on, we're going to find out".

The roar of Nancy's scattergun being returning fire from the man who had fired at Jack Cunningham, bounced off the canyon walls with enough authority to make the four remaining men to give up and ride out. Once clear of the canyon, and sure they were out of sight of the Marshal, the four began to circle back to the north. About two hours into the ride they came upon an outcropping of some size that gave good cover from both their back trail, and at the same time allowed them to see anyone who might come in from the north. A small fire was built, and they began to take turns at night guard. All four men, heavily armed, and alert, were determined to reconnect with the main body. They may have been routed once, but they had been careless. This time would be different.

Several hundred yards away, three riders sat shadowed from sight by a small group of trees. Marshal Cunningham handed Elk the glass and pointed to the outcropping. "They just pulled into that outcropping ahead RE. About three hundred yards and to the right a bit". Elk nodded, then handed the glass to his mother.

"Be dark in about half an hour. We'll move in then. A shame though. It didn't have to be this way".

"Some people are just plain stupid son, but in this case I think it might be greed, or maybe fear of the man they work for that's driving them. In any case, we either turn them back, or leave them for the birds. After what happened to Oliver, I don't much care one way or the other".

"Me either mother. We might as well rest a bit, while we

have a chance. When the time comes, we will have to walk up there anyway".

Dismounting, Elk led the horses back a few feet and looping the reins together draped them over the branch of a small bush. He knew this was unnecessary because these were Indian ponies, and would stay put even without being tied. Now dark, he started back and was about halfway there when he saw Jack leaning against a tree. The Marshal help up his hand for Elk to be quiet and then motioned to another tree a short distance away. Nancy was setting on the ground with her back up against the tree asleep. The darkness shrouded her to the point that she would have to be almost stepped on to be discovered. Cunningham pulled his Dragoon and pointed to the outcropping. Elk nodded his agreement, and together they stepped out of the cover of the trees into the darkness.

About fifty yards from the outcropping they split up, Elk moving to the right, and Cunningham to the left. Moving silently, the young Marshal was able to work his way within five feet of the man guarding the camp. Finding the man asleep he eased up behind him and covering the man's mouth jerked his head back and slit his throat. He had just eased the man to the ground when the three shots rang out into the darkness. There was no mistaking the sound of that big Dragoon fortyfour Cunningham carried. Cunningham called out. "That's it Elk, I'm comin' out". Stepping out of the outcropping he holstered his pistol and together they started back toward the trees. "God, RE, I hate stupidity. The bastards had a chance to ride out. Now their vulture food".

Nancy met them at the tree line holding her scattergun at the hip. "Why didn't you wake me son"?

"You didn't need to be part of that mother. Let's go, this is getting rough and I want to be in camp before noon tomorrow".

Twenty two

Keith Tully, (Known to those around him, as Irish Bob) had rented everything the liveryman had except for the three horses that were in a fenced in area at the back of the shop. Calling over one of his henchmen, he told the man to rent those as well. "They're small, but we can use them to carry the supplies. I don't want this carriage loaded down to the point where we get stuck in the mud somewhere". The man disappeared into the shop, only to return a short time later empty handed, with the news the three weren't for rent, but had been brought in this morning for customers who had not yet arrived.

Sensing trouble, he decided to find out for himself just who these customers might be. "Bring the man out here, I want to talk to him. I think I already know the answers he will give me, but I need to hear it anyway". Like an obedient servant the man nodded and brought out the liveryman ushering him up to the side of the carriage.

"Yes sir, you want to see me"?

Smiling, Tully lit a cigar, leaned back against the seat, and sat looking at the man. Mister, we have a need for those extra horses you have penned out back. Suppose you just hustle back there and get them ready for me? We'll need to have them rigged for pack animals, so no need to worry yourself with the rest of the rigging".

Can't do that mister. Them ponies ain't mine to rent anyway. Came in here early this mornin'. Brought in by some Shoshone braves who said they was for folks that would be along directly".

"Shoshone, you say. Aren't they the Indians that are north of here"?

"Yep, the very ones. Paid me in gold too. Now, that doesn't happen to often around here. Anyway I got to honor my business practice. I'm sorry, but I can't let you have them".

Again, Tully smiled. "Think nothing of it my friend, business is business. We'll just be on our way. Oh, by the way, this gold, was it coin or dust"?
Well, it weren't neither. It was just small smooth pieces if gold. Looked to me like it had been cut off a larger piece. Gold is gold, so I don't much care how it comes".
"Indeed. Well, thank you friend. We'll be on our way, and I assure you these horses, and this carriage, will be returned to you none the worse for wear in a very few days".
The liveryman waved and returned to his shop leaving Tully and his gang to ponder what they had just heard. Motioning for his men to gather around, he said. "Well gentlemen, you heard the man. I do believe we are on the right trail. Now, suppose we just go and see what kind of job our young man did in hiring all those bad men from Texas. I would like very much to get through with this business and return to civilization. Keep a sharp eye out for trouble. This has been far too easy, up to now"

Twenty three

The lodge meeting lasted about two hours. The young men were asked to leave, and without revealing the location, the Chief told the Elders of the gold. Several of the Elders rose to give their views on the situation as was the custom, but to the man, they all knew what had to be done, gold or no gold. The problem was, that there were so many coming against them. It was voiced by some that this was, something that should be left up to the law, but those few were reminded that the law was already here. This kind of trouble had visited this camp before and many years ago a blood oath had been taken that it would never happen again. The meeting ended leaving only the Chief, Elk, Cunningham, and Nancy sitting around the small fire in the lodge. Cunningham noticed the look on the Chief's face and said, "RE, we got some plannin' to do. Let's go, I got some ideas".

Elk had been making small talk with his father and without looking up said, "Be with you in a bit Jack".

"NOW, RE! You're workin' for me. Get off your ass and get out here".

Elks head snapped around and his eyes met those of the Marshal. "Now RE, right now". And the Marshal turned and walked out of the lodge.

Elk excused himself, and uncoiling like a spring, stomped through the door after Cunningham. The Marshal was now several yards away and Elk had to hurry to catch up. Taking hold of Cunningham's elbow, he stopped him making no effort to hide his anger, and the smile on Cunningham's face didn't help either "Listen Jack, Marshal or no Marshal, I was talking to my father in there, and what you did just now was just plain rude. Who the hell do you think you are anyway"?

"Oh for crap sake RE, couldn't you see the look on your

father's face. He didn't want to be talkin' to you, he was just bein' polite. He wanted to talk to Nancy. My God boy, are you ever thick headed. Now let's go. I don't know about you, but, I for one am starved, and tired, and dirty, or don't you people ever bath"?

It was now Elk's turn to smile. "Why yes, Jack, we bath right in that creek over there. Usually in front of the whole camp. I would have suggested it before now, but I ain't at all sure your stuff could stand the cold water".

The creek Elk was referring to was located about twenty yards from the lodges, and in the open. Looking around, Cunningham made a decision that caused the young Marshal to roar with laughter. "I'll wait till it gets dark, and don't be makin' no more comments about my stuff. I just like a little privacy is all".

Meanwhile, Tully, and his gang from Chicago had met up with the now fortysix remaining outlaws from Texas, the lookout had warned the leader of the approaching men, and he, and his lieutenants stood waiting for them as they came through the small draw in the canyon. Seeing the carriage and the way the riders were dressed brought a smile to his face. "Ever see anything like that before Stan? These folks are downright purty".

The man who had been sent by Tully to hire this bunch stepped up beside him. "Mister, that man riding in the carriage that you call pretty, is Mr. Keith Tully, the man I work for. He is one of the chief bosses from Chicago, and he will pull your damn teeth out and stuff them up your ass one at a time, if you're not careful. Walk very softly around him".

Tully stopped the carriage in the middle of the camp and his men immediately began spreading out in a semi circle around him. Remaining seated, he looked around at the camp and after lighting a cigar, stepped out of the carriage. "Looks good Ronald, any trouble"?

"Had a bit of a problem at first Mr. Tully, it became necessary to make other arrangements. I believe we now have what you requested. Pointing to the young outlaw standing next to him, he said, "This gentleman here calls himself Smith. He is the leader of this bunch, and most follow his direction".

Wiping his hands on his jeans, Smith stepped forward and stuck out his hand. "Nice to meet you Mr. Tully".

Tully looked at the dirty hand of the young man and taking out his handkerchief, he draped it over his hand and shook the young man's hand. The strength in Tully's hand caused the outlaw to grimace just a bit. Still holding his hand in the viselike grip, he began to explain why they were there.

"Mr. Smith, we have come a very long way to this God forsaken place on a matter of importance. This is a dangerous venture, but when it is completed you and your associates here will be paid more money than you would normally earn in a lifetime. For that, I expect you to obey my orders, or the orders of those I send to you, without question. Carry those orders out and we will get along just fine. If you fail to carry them out I will have you killed and replace you with someone who will. Do you understand, Mr. Smith"?

Tully's grip had turned Smith's hand white. He shook it several times and began rubbing his fingers. "Mr. Smith, did you hear me"?

Smith flared up". Hell yes I heard you! You bast…" The business end of Ronald's pistol stopped him cold. "I mean yes Mr. Tully, anything you want".

Tully slapped the young man on the back. "That's the spirit young man. Now suppose we get down to business". Tully turned on his heel and began giving orders to his men.

Still rubbing his hand, Smith turned to Ronald. "Is he always like that"?

"For as long as I can remember. Has a strong grip doesn't

he"?

"Damn near broke my hand. What happens now"?

"Whatever he wants. I suspect we are going to ride north. Better get your boy's ready to move out".

Pete and Zac pushed hard, and the evening of the second day found the two lying on their stomachs of the canyon rim watching about sixty men through their glasses. Pete had pulled his fifty caliber rifle from the sheath where it normally rested just below his right leg, and was now adjusting the sights on the big gun. A weapon meant for bear, or buffalo, or other big game, and Zac had seen Pete use it for that on occasion, but he had also seen him use it the way he was getting ready to use it now. As a man killer. The old man grimaced, remembering the damage it had done on several previous occasions. "That's a hell of a big war party down there son, you sure you know what you're doin'"?

Pete had been sighting down the barrel, but eased back, and turning to look at the old man, he said, 'We'll know in a minute". Looking back once again he clicked the hammer back, sighted for just a second and squeezed the trigger. The big bullet found its mark before the sound of the rifle was even heard. The downward force of the slug slammed Ronald in the breastbone knocking him to the ground as if he had been pole axed. The outlaw slid backward several feet and lay still. The second shot caught another one of Tully's men just above the right ear blowing off the top of his head, and sending his hat some fifteen feet in the air. Zac, watching the camp diving for cover and firing at anything and everything looked over at a smiling Pete. "Damn, you sure as hell got the ball rollin' now. We better move, and quick". Pete nodded, and together they faded into the underbrush like ghosts.

The boom of the big fifty sent the entire camp grabbing iron and diving for cover. Sixty men began firing and it took several minutes for Tully and his men to quiet them down. Once done, Tully gave orders for the ridge to be scouted and those who had done the shooting to be brought back to face him. Smith, hearing the order walked over to where Tully was still crouching behind the carriage. "Mr. Tully, ain't no use sendin' nobody up there now. That shot you heard was from a fifty caliber and whoever was using' it, is long gone now".

Tully looked at Smith unable to contain his rage at being shot at with all of these men around him. "Listen you ignorant son of a bitch. No one tries to kill me and just rides away. When I say I want someone on that ridge, they go to the ridge. Now get your ass away from me before I decide I don't need you anymore. Bury my two men, and do it right, or you will be in the grave with them".

By the time Tully had finished, Smith was visibly shaking and all he could get out was, "Yes sir, Mr. Tully. Right away, Mr. Tully". Turning back to his other men, Tully shouted another order. "Get this bunch ready, we're moving out now! And, I want men watching both ahead and behind for whoever is doing this. Leave this carriage and find me a horse, we need to make some time".

As the bunch headed north, they were accompanied by two lone riders, determined to side track their plans.

Twenty four

Elk found Jack Cunningham sitting by himself away from camp, aimlessly poking a stick into a small fire. As he approached, the Marshal looked up. "Have a seat RE, we need to talk".

Elk sat down and leaned back against the log. "What's on your mind, Jack"?

Cunningham pointed to the camp. "That. That's what is on my mind. All of these women and kids. These bastards comin' won't give a damn about them. They'll gun them down like they are nothing at all, and I aim to do something about that, I've thought it over and I'll be leaving before daylight. Zac and Pete are already out there, and, knowing them two, the ball is already rollin'. I aim to join em' and keep it going, or at least do what I can to run this trash off".

"Hold on there, Jack, this is rough country, and you don't know it. To do what you say, is not only dangerous, I'm not so sure it is even a good idea".

Uh huh, well, hell, son, you don't need me here. You and the Chief will look after the camp. You know, as well as I do, that you can't send out a war party after these bastards. They might slip by them and then the camp would be at their mercy. No, the men have to stay in camp and fight from here, if they hit. Your job is to see that it stays protected, and you don't need me for that, so, I'm going out there and do what I do best. Enforce the law".

Over the years, Elk had watched his friend do just that too. He had seen Jack Cunningham stand against odds that would have made lesser men quit their office. He had seen him draw, and fire, that big Dragoon of his in defense of those he had sworn to defend when he accepted his office as Chief Marshal of the territory. Elk smiled as he remembered walking by the circle jail in Crawfordsville, Indiana one time and overhearing one of the inmates comment. "Cunningham? Yeah, I know Cunningham, had a run in with him. He is one, tough, son of a bitch".

"You know you can get yourself killed out there don't you? These outfits we're up against aren't just a bunch of cowboys out trying to get easy money. These boy's mean business and if they have brought in men from Texas to boot we may be in for a war".

The Marshal pulled out one of his store bought cigarettes, lit it, and blew the smoke out through his nose. "To tell you the truth, Elk, in this job, I hadn't expected to live this long. Remember when I went up against them two boys that were holed up in Yountsville that time? Thought for sure that was it. On the other hand, I have been at this for quite a spell now and I ain't exactly intending to call nobody out for gunplay. This is dirty business and I don't care if these boys even see me. I'm the law and what I do out here is my business. That makes anything I do legal and I aim to put a hurt on these boys they won't forget. So, I'll be leavin' before sunup. I'd appreciate it if you would give me the loan of a rifle though. Most likely won't get close enough to use this Dragoon of mine".

It was late by the time Elk returned to Cunningham's fire with the rifle and ammunition. Jack was already on his bed roll and watched as the young deputy approached his fire. Setting up he leaned back against the log and lit another cigarette. "RE, we been pards for a spell now, and I'm asking you to stay here in camp and keep these folks safe from this trash. Ain't any use in you comin' out with me. I know what I'm getting' into here and I can take care of myself. Deal"?

"Reckon you're right, Jack. See you when you get back". Setting the rifle down he shook hands with his old friend. "See you when this is over, Jack". He turned and started back the way he had come. Cunningham smiled and turned in. Daylight found him, and his Indian pony headed into the mountains alone.

Elk returned to camp and went directly to his father's lodge. Entering, he was surprised to find the Chief still up at this hour. "Father, you are still up"?

"Come, son, and sit beside me. We have much to talk about". Elk sat down and waited for his father to speak. "What of you friend Marshal Cunningham? Is he going out alone against these men"?

"He is, father. Jack feels that he is not needed here, and that he can be of more help by striking at them before they get here. It is his thinking that he, and Zac, and Pete, just may be able to turn them around. At least that bunch that has come here from Texas".

"And, what of you? What are your plans? Are you going to let your friend the Marshal go out there alone in country that he knows nothing about? You were raised here Running Elk, and you know how hard this country can be. Jack is our friend, but he is white, and doesn't know the Indian way. He means well, but the odds are too great for him now. No, you must go and help him. That is our way". Elk started to speak, but the Chief held up his hand for silence. "No, you are not needed here now. We will take care of the women and children without you. We are not in this valley for no reason. Do you not think that all those years ago, when the people first came here that we did not consider our enemies? Over the years we have defended this valley many times against those who would come against us and these men are no different. Go to your friend and let us take care of this business that is coming". He had finished, and Elk knew that was the final word. To argue against his father would be useless. The young Marshal rose to his feet and walked from the lodge. Thirty minutes later found him on Marshal Cunningham's back trail. Having ridden south for most of the day the Marshal had picked a night camp well hidden from view. Knowing that even a small fire could spell trouble, he would be making cold camps until this mess was cleared up. For a great many years he had relied on his senses to warn him of not only impending danger, but of anything out of the ordinary. They had saved his life on more than one occasion and just now those same senses had awakened him. He eased out of his bed roll and pulling his Dragoon, moved deeper into the brush where his field of vision would allow him to see anyone approaching, dark or not. A stranger meaning no harm would hail the camp. An enemy would not, and if that were the case he could be in real trouble. "You know Jack, I have never figured out just how it is you do that. You sure you ain't part Indian"? Snapping his head around Cunningham found himself looking into the eyes of his Deputy sitting not three feet away.

Cunningham wasn't smiling. "RE, what the hell is wrong with you? I could have shot you just now. What are you doing out here anyway"?

"Came to help. Father thought you might get yourself in trouble out here all alone. Mentioned something about you bein' afraid of the dark. Sent me to hold your hand".

"Uh huh. How long did it take you to sneak up on me like that"?

"Quite a while actually. I've seen you do that wakin' up stuff before, and I wanted to see if I could best you. Stepped on something a second ago and you came alive. Pretty amazing stuff Jack".

"Yeah, well as long as you got me up, what say we make us some coffee? I don't like this cold camp a bit. I don't work well without coffee. How far off do you think that bunch is"?

"Not sure, they could be anywhere. One thing is sure though. If they have been hit by Zac and Pete, they are going to be jumpy, and that makes them dangerous. Unless I miss my guess, they will have scouts out far enough to give them advance warning. A gunshot carries a good distance in these mountains and Tully isn't going to care how many die as long as he gets what he is after. So, we best be careful, from here on in".

Cunningham took a sip of coffee and lit a cigarette letting the smoke drift out through his nostrils. RE, this is bad business. There has never been a time as long as I remember that I have set out to bushwhack anyone. Bad or good, I have always given the other man a fair chance. This time we don't have that choice. There are so many of these bastards that we need to hit them whenever and wherever we can. This Irish Bob as he is called is a bad hombre, and we need to kill the son of a bitch before this goes too far. We hit him, and the rest of them will turn tail and run".

Elk poured the remaining coffee on the small fire, and spread the ashes around stepping on what coals remained. "Yeah, well let's get to it. I don't intend on letting them get to the town or the gold, and if that means killing them from hiding, then that's the way it will be. This was their choice and I intend to soak their sorry asses in blood, and soon".

Daylight found them working their way carefully along the ridges. Stopping ever so often and using the glasses to try and spot Tully and his gang. It was about noon when Cunningham spotted the first of them riding cautiously through a narrow canyon. He handed the glass to Elk and dismounted. "This is as good as anyplace to get things started. We can hit and run". The deputy nodded and they set themselves up so they would have a clear field of fire without being seen from below. Waiting until there were about fifteen riders in the canyon they lined up on the last two in line and were about to squeeze of the rounds when the roar of Pete's big fifty caliber rolled off the canyon walls. Even from this distance the Marshal could see the spray of blood as the big round exploded the head of the last man in line, knocking him from his horse and sending the rest of those in the canyon into panicked flight back the way they had come. By this time Zac's rifle and both Elk and Cunningham's rifles had come into play and more men began littering the canyon floor. Pete's fifty caliber roared time and again sending outlaws to hell where they belonged. The firing lasted no more than three or four minutes, but the damage had been done, and more than that, a deadly message had been sent to Tully, and his henchmen from Chicago. Eleven men now lay dead on the canyon floor, men who had thought this to be easy money now lay at the very feet of the gangster from Chicago. When the shooting had started Tully had stepped back into the shadows of the canyon wall and watched as Pete's big fifty tore through his men. Bullets rained down from above and both sides cutting the men to pieces. A clear picture came to him then and he knew what had to be done if he were to ever see any of the gold they had come so far to take. There seemed to be no more than three of four guns firing now and his men were dropping like flies. What would the results have been if there had been ten or even twenty firing on them from above? The problem was numbers, there were just more men here than he needed to get the job done. They were easy targets and now had become useless to his cause. A change had to be made and quick if he wanted to come out of this alive let alone get his hands on the gold. There was a couple of ways to handle this and to his credit, at least this time he decided to take the high road. When the firing stopped he stepped out of the shadows and telling the men to stay where they were began to speak.

"Men, I have made a drastic error in judgment here and I find I must apologize for that error. It just isn't right for me to expect you men who rode in here from Texas to continue on with this effort so I am releasing you from your commitment and sending you back to your homes or wherever it is you came from. Please see Mr. Singer here for whatever pay you have coming and we will call it a day. Thank you for your efforts on our behalf". Taking up the reins of his horse he mounted and started back the way they had come.

The cowboys began to come out of hiding and stood staring at him as he rode by unable to believe what they had just heard. The young leader of the cowboys stepped out blocking the road. "Where the hell do you think you're going? We got us a deal here and there ain't no turnin' tail and runnin'".

Tully relaxed and looked at the man. "Mr. Smith. These men lying dead here are a testament to the fact that these people do not want us here. In the last three days we have lost more than fifteen men and have not even had an opportunity to speak with the people we came here to do business with. That tells me we need to make some changes in the way we do things and these changes do not include you or your men. Now, if you will see the paymaster we can conclude our business and all be on our way".

Smith backed up a few steps and stood with legs about shoulder width apart and hands resting on the two tied down pistols hung low on his hips. "You son of a bitch. Do you think you can have us ride all the way from Texas to Wyoming with the promise of riches and then turn around and send us back just like that? We were promised more money than we could make in a lifetime and all we have been paid so far is blood and death. Your fancy speech and fancy clothes don't mean nothin' out here mister. Now, get your ass off that horse and let's get things straightened out before I blow you to hell".

While Smith had been making his play Tully had calmly lit one of his cigars and sat looking at the man. When Smith finished talking Tully made one quick move and put a small clean hole in the middle of Smiths forehead. Smiths eyes crossed while watching his own blood squirt six or eight inches away before falling dead where he stood. Reaching into his saddle bags he pulled out a bound leather bag throwing it to the ground, and spoke once again to the cowboys. "Men, thank you again for your service, there is ten thousand dollars in cash in that bag. Split it among yourselves any way you want. Go home men, your job here is done". He turned his horse and headed for the rail station in Cheyenne with death on his mind. He had never lost a battle and this would be no exception. He knew he needed to fight this one in his own way and eventually on his own ground. The gold had now become secondary. This had now become personal between him and the bitch from Crawfordsville and her half breed son. He smiled at the thought of slitting Marshal Cunningham's throat.

Twenty five

The cowboys from Texas as well as the gangsters from Indianapolis and Chicago had scattered in all directions trying to get away from the murderous fire from above. Seeking shelter behind rocks, logs or anything else they could find desperately trying to stay alive. Zac stood on the opposite rim and held his rifle above his head for the four of them to hold fire. Elk and Cunningham watched as the two mounted and disappeared into the woods behind them then eased up to the edge of the rim and watched through glasses to see what would happen next. They knew they had spooked this bunch, but didn't know how bad it was. When Tully stepped out from the shadows and swung himself into the saddle Elk centered him in his rifle sites and was about to squeeze of the round when Jack touched his shoulder. "Hold on pard there is some kind of disagreement going down there. See the way that cowboy is standin'? We're about to see gunplay here. This may be over before it even gets started. Trouble among thieves, I love it". They watched as Tully pulled a cigar from his coat, light it and calmly blow smoke into the air, and as the cowboy backed up a few paces and spread his legs. Neither saw Tully move in any way and did not realize he had shot the other man until they heard the shot and saw the man fall on his face. "R.E., did you see him draw and fire"?
"No, just heard the shot and saw the man fall".
"That was no sleeve gun. Looks to me like a 38 or 40 caliber. If that's right this is one dangerous son of a bitch. Shoot him R.E, NOW"!
Elk raised the rifle once again but a few seconds to late, Tully had turned his horse and was riding out of the canyon at a trot with all of his men close behind. Jack studied the man for a few seconds before he spoke. "He's paying them boys off in cash R.E. we may have broken this thing up

before it got started".

Pete and Zac were working their way along the ridge in the cover of the trees when they heard the cowboys riding through the canyon. Thinking they might have another chance to discourage this bunch they tied off the horses and belly crawled to the edge overlooking the trail below. Pete pulled out the glass and scanned the line of men below. "I, they ain't even lookin' around or nothin. The pack animals are loaded and all rifles are booted. I think they are sendin' us a message. Looks to me like they are ridin' out for good. What do you want to do"?

Zac took the glass and studied the men below. "You may be right. There is no way of tellin' though. Put one of them fifty rounds about twenty yards in front of them and let's see what happens. If there is fight in em' that will do it for sure". The big fifty caliber bucked against his shoulder and dirt sprayed sixty feet in front of the lead horse making it buck, causing the rider no little effort in controlling the animal. He expected the men to dismount and return fire as before, but this time they kept to the trail and continued on raising their hands above their head. Zac spit a stream of tobacco juice over the edge of the canyon and shook his head. Their done, them boys are headed back to where they belong. Spect they ain't a bad lot at that. Just got in with that trash out here from the east".

Zac heard the call of a hunting hawk and looked up to see Elk standing on the ridge directly across from them. He began making sign and Zac answered in kind Pete got most but not all of what Elk had said and ask about the rest. "Elk say's he and Cunningham are goin' to follow them cowboys a ways. Say's there are enough of em' to cause trouble if they were to swing around and come against the people at the village. Says he wants us to head for the village and keep a watchful eye on things. What do you say Pete"?

"Sounds about right to me, I figure them folks from the city has had enough of us savage people to last them a lifetime, gold or no gold. I would like to spend some time with mother before she goes back east anyway". Zac laughed out loud causing Pete to frown a bit. "What's so funny anyway"?

"Son, besides your real father Nancy has never loved any man more than she does that Indian Chief runnin' that village. If you think for one minute she is goin' to leave him again you might want to reconsider. Haven't you seen the way they look at each other? Wouldn't surprise me if they don't start a whole new family. And don't look so serious boy, love is a wonderful thing. Or have you forgot"?

"No you old skunk I haven't forgot. How could anyone ever forget Fawn? When I close my eyes I still see her beauty and feel her smooth skin against my chest. But the Chief and Ma, a bit old for that sort of thing ain't they"?

"Never sell love short son. Powerful stuff, love".

Marshal Cunningham and his deputy followed the cowboys for over two days and turned back only when they were sure the men were indeed headed out of the territory.

"Damn strange R.E., them boys turnin tail like that. Guess they just had enough of Tully and that bunch".

"Who wouldn't? The man is a piece of crap fit for nothing. Everything he stands for has death written all over it. Men like that live in a different world than the rest of us. Thing is, you got to get in the gutter with em' if you are goin' to beat em'. I for one am glad they're gone. You going to finish this when you get home"? "Truth is there ain't much I can do about any of this. It's a shame about Oliver, but he is the one who got himself into this mess. Your mother settled her score with McFarland, her gold is safe and Irish Bob is headed back to Indianapolis or Chicago and that's pretty much the end of it as far as the law is concerned".

"Uh huh, you figure there is going to be a wedding Jack"?
Cunningham smiled slapped Elk on the back. "Deputy,
ain't a doubt I my mind. Hell, you may have a brother or
sister before this over".

Zac and Pete entered the village about sundown and went
straight to the creek washing off the trail dust and some of
the bad memories of the past few days. Nancy had cooked
the evening meal, something that Zac's nose told him even
before he headed for the creek. She was starting to clean
things up when he approached the cooking fire. "Hey sis,
ain't you going to save some of that fine cookin' of yours
for a couple of hungry men"?

Looking up she smiled then walked over and took Zac by
the hand. "For you old friend I would start cooking all over
again. Where is that son of mine"?

"He's comin', and mighty hungry as well. You may need to
prod him a bit to bring him around Nancy. We been on a
long and hard road for the past few years. Changes a man
to do that sort of thing. Makes him hard of heart and
trustin' of no one. Just be yourself and he will come
around. Just needs his mother's love I reckon".

Zac had been right. Pete had come to the fire to eat, but was
quiet and withdrawn at first. Nancy sat by him and began to
speak of the hound and the mules they had come west with
the first time. The talk lasted long into the night with each
one telling things of the heart until sometime in the early
hours of the morning.

Twenty six

In the late eighteen eighties a new and terrible weapon came into its own. The Spencer repeater, a sliding or pump action shotgun that would later revolutionize the shotgun industry and eventually all but do away with the old double barrel shotgun.

Tully and his men made the ride back to Cheyenne but instead of boarding the train for Indianapolis or Chicago, checked into the hotel. He then went to the telegraph office sending a message to Chicago. After that was done he purchased some new clothes and headed for the local bath, then instructed his men to do the same. The local merchants liked the way these men spent money and soon became accustomed to seeing them in town. It didn't take long before mutual friendships developed to the point that almost all were on first name basis. This then became part of Tullies plan, something that over the years he had become very adept at. Using good and honest people to his own evil advantage. When his plans were carried out and he had succeeded in whatever he had used people for it was often many months before those used would find out. Some never did. Criminal or no, Tully was a very resourceful man.

It took no more than three days for word of the gang's whereabouts to get back to the village and Marshal Cunningham. He and Elk left early on the fourth day headed for Cheyenne to settle the problem once and for all. Unbeknown to both Marshals Pete and Zac left that same morning to back whatever action the Marshals took. When Jack and Elk arrived in town the action fell far short of what they had imagined. As they rode past the hotel Tully and several of his men sat lounging on the porch smoking cigars and talking to the townspeople. Tully took the time to wave and then turned back to the conversation.

Marshal Cunningham waved back then swore. "Did you see that R.E.? this thing is getting' worse all the time. Hell, I just can't go over there and start killin' people for crying out loud. The way everyone is dressed I'd shoot half the town by mistake. I need a drink and time to work this out". Tying their horses off in front of the Cheyenne House they walked inside and ordered whisky. The bartender didn't want to serve Elk and said so. Jack took his dragoon out and set it on the bar. "You get that bottle over here and damn fast before I put the barrel of this thing where the sun don't shine and pull the trigger". He poured Elk a shot and taking the bottle walked over and sat down at a table in the back of the room. They hadn't been there more than a few minutes when the door opened and Tully walked in. taking a few seconds to look over the room he spotted the marshals and walked over to their table.

"Well gentleman, we meet again. I am told it is customary for strangers in this town to let the local law officers know what one is about. I haven't really been here long enough to talk much to the local sheriff but am quite sure that is sufficient, nevertheless I thought it prudent to let you two know as well. Yes, well having done that I will be on my way". Tully tipped his hat and turned to leave.

"Just a minute smart ass. I have a couple of questions". The acid in Jack Cunningham's voice froze Tully in his tracks and he turned back around. The Marshals nostrils were flared and the skin on his face was drawn tight with hate for this man. Tully looked into eyes that just now were nothing more than slits. The half breed setting next to the Marshal had both hands resting on the table and was setting as still as stone. Tully was as close to death as he had ever been and he knew it. He tried to make his usual glib remark but his voice cracked under the strain of the moment. "Why yes Marshal, what's your pleasure"?

"You're a piece of shit Tully, your mother was no doubt

some kind of an filthy animal and what are you and your garbage still doing in this good town".

The insult turned Tullies face white with rage and spittle sprayed as he spoke. "I am surprised at your tone Marshal. Actually, I have decided to stay here in this lovely town and rest a bit before returning home. I trust that meets with your approval".

Cunningham didn't blink. "I know you carry a sidearm for murdering folks Tully. I want you to go for it now. I'm going to send you to hell and I aim to do it now you son of a whore".

Tully had regained his composure and looked at Elk. "Young man I assume you to be this idiots deputy. If you would be so kind I would like for you to lift the sides of my jacket so the good Marshal here can see that I am not armed. I know you would like nothing better than to murder me Marshal but we are not going to let that happen. At least not today".

Elk didn't move. "Tell you what Tully, suppose you just reach up and pull the sides of your jacket out real slow so the good Marshal here can see if you are armed. A bit risky though as the Marshal has had a drink or two. He might just shoot you anyway".

Tully reached for his jacket and Cunningham picked up the Dragoon, thumbed the hammer back and smiled. "Go ahead Keith, let's have a look".

Tully pulled back his coat and smiled. "Well Marshal, I might as well head on back. I can see that you are busy here upholding the law. It seems that bottle of whisky there is pretty common among lawmen. I guess that's where the saying "courage in a bottle" comes from".

Through the insults the Marshal hadn't said a word. The hammer was still pulled back on his Dragoon and it was still aimed at Tullies chest. This time when he spoke there was no doubt in anyone's mind Tully was as close to death as he had ever been. This was especially clear to Tully himself. "Take your jacket off and roll up your sleeves Keith, I want to see if you are holding a wrist gun".

Taking off his jacket he folded it neatly and draped it over the back of a chair and rolled up his sleeves. "Now take your pants off and lay them on that chair there. I want to see if you've got a boot gun". Elk's laughter brought out the fury in Tully.

"You're a bastard Marshal, you know that? I'll pull my pants leg up but I will undress for no man. You son of a bitch, who do you think you are"?

Cunningham moved his hand slightly and the big Dragoon jumped. Those in the room dove for the floor and Tully himself thought he had been shot. As it was the Marshal had blown a hole in the jacket Tully had so carefully lain on the chair. "Keith, the next time I pull this trigger you will be in hell. Now get your pants off".

"Look Marshal, why don't I just put my foot up on this chair and pull my pant leg up. I don't have a boot gun I can assure you. I do need to get back to my business and I can see I have made a mistake even coming over here".

"Pants off Keith, I'm tired of askin'".

Elk spoke up making the situation even worse. "Hell Jack, just shoot his fat ass".

Tully panicked a bit. "Look Marshal, when we got to town all the general store had was common clothes. I was unable to find underwear that was suitable so I didn't buy any. Actually I'm not even wearing any underwear at all. So you see it wouldn't be proper for me to undress in this place".

Elk broke out in laughter as did everyone else in the room. "Get your damn pants off Keith before I shoot you. You ain't got nothin' we haven't seen before. I mean now Keith".

Tully unbuckled his belt letting his pants drop around his ankles, stepped out of them and stood naked except for his shirt and tie. Marshal Cunningham leaned around the table a bit and looked at Tullies ankles, then his pants. "Damn Keith you need to do a better job of cleanin' up after you go to the pot. You got skid marks in them new pants. Look at that Elk, skid marks".

Tully had had enough, he grabbed his pants and started to put them back on when the Marshal stopped him. "I've seen more than enough of you Keith go outside to dress. Deputy would you please walk Keith to the door"?

When Tully stepped outside everyone on the walk stopped and stared. His only comment was, "You and your families are all dead".

"Uh huh. You better get them pants on Tully. Those kids are looking at your privates". Elk returned to the table to find Jack leaned back in his chair sipping his drink as if nothing had happened. "He's going to kill you, said so too".

"That was the whole idea R.E., I want him and the rest of that scum to come on and get the ball rollin' god I hate people like that. Guess we better keep an eye on them".

"Jack after what you just did you better sleep with both eyes open. The kids out front were pointing and laughing at his privates".

"Yeah, did look like he had been in cold water".

For the next two weeks the suits from the east began drifting into town by the twos and threes and there was no mistaking the long covered gun cases. Elk and Cunningham had been eating at the diner and stepped out in time to see more men step off the train and walk across the tracks toward the hotel. "You know what this is all about don't you Jack? These bastards are planning to hit my father's camp. Women and children are going to die over this and I am not going to let that happen. How do you want to handle this?

"Ain't a hell of a lot we can do about it R.E., they ain't

breakin' no laws. There is no law against having guns and if we were to go to the judge over this he would turn us down for sure. Pete and Zac are in town and I know they have been watching this bunch same as us. Might be a good idea if they were to ride on back and warn your father about these going's on. Might want to get them headed that way before nightfall". Elk nodded his agreement and stepped out into the street. "Soon as you find them head on back, we might have to move on short notice". Again the young Marshal nodded his understanding. Cunningham pulled out one of his store bought cigarettes and lit it. Blowing the smoke out through his nose he sat down and leaned his chair back up against the wall. From here he had a good view of the Cheyenne House and the bordello next door. If they were going to move this night he would know it.

Twenty seven

The Shoshone camp was about forty miles to the north and Running Elk had done all he could to prepare the people for what he knew would be a blood bath if this situation wasn't brought under control. This was nothing like the wars of the past where brave men faced each other in combat. Even a hated enemy showed and was due respect, but this was different. There was no respect here and the motivation for this was nothing more than greed by a bunch who had no qualms about killing even women and children. Blood was going to run and many families would be wiped out completely. Having waited as long as he could the Chief decided to move the entire camp to the mountains spreading out the camp at least giving the people a chance to run and hide in the rocks and caves if need be.

Smoke curled up through the hole in the top of the meeting lodge as the Chief began to explain their situation and his decision to move the camp. Seeing the disapproval on the faces of most of the elders present he fell silent allowing those who chose to speak an opportunity to do so. One after the other men rose voicing their opposition to moving the camp in the face of upcoming trouble.

"It is not the way of the Shoshone people to run from battle. We have always stood and faced our enemies like men. What you are asking is the coward's way. How much stronger can this enemy be than those we have faced in the past? Let them come and taste the Shoshone lance. We have as many rifles as the white man. Let them learn to respect us as men, not rabbits".

Running Elk could see the both futility of his efforts and the pride of his people. It made him proud and sad at the same time.

"My brothers, I have been your chief for many years and my love of our people is as strong as any man here. Hear me when I tell you that if we do not move our families to a safer place we will suffer much blood and destruction. Some of our families will be no more. We will stand and see our women and children scattered about like firewood and I fear their shadows will walk this valley forever". "My brothers, I stand firm on my word as chief and we will move our camp to safer ground".

A young brave stood throwing his rifle on the ground in front of the chief. "I Angry Wolf of the Shoshone say you have become as an old woman! Perhaps we should get you a dress and soft food to dip your old fingers in. As for me I will stand and fight these white strangers. If I die then I will die like a man of the Shoshone is intended"!

The chief reached over and picking up the young warriors rifle and held it out to him. His eyes burning into the younger man and though angry he spoke so softly all there had to strain to hear him. "I did not say we would not fight our enemy. I said that we were moving the camp to safer ground to protect our women and children. If you do not wish to hear my plan you are free to leave now and fight alone at a place of your choosing. If you wish to stand with your brothers you will sit and listen to the plan. Make your decision now or leave the lodge".

The young man took back his rifle and sat down finding himself unable to meet any of those eyes that were now on him.

Nodding his approval the chief began to outline his plan. "My idea is this. The scouts will be out and we will know in advance when this these men get close. The camp will be left just as it is. Lodges with cooking fires burning, and the ponies will be left at the creek as they now are. We will move the women and children to the small plateau that is just below the caves. If they are attacked the caves will give them protection and it will take but a few warriors to defend them. The men of the camp will place themselves among the rocks as we did during our last attack. I know, that was many years ago, but it worked then and I believe it will work now. We will wait until the enemy rides into the camp and then open fire. Marshal Cunningham, Zacaria, Pete and my son will be involved in the fight and I have no doubt they will surprise these men that wish to do us harm. The plan is simple but strong. Do you approve of it"?

"Angry Wolf, the people will need you to place your braves among the rocks as best you see fit. You are the strongest and quickest as we witnessed when your father and his braves saved Nancy Weliever and her son from being murdered many years ago. It will be good to place warriors within rifle range all the way up to the plateau. That way the fire will rain from all over the side of the mountain. I want these men to feed the birds and ride only one way on this day".

Angry Wolf stood facing the Chief. It will be as you say Running Elk. Letting out a yell, he raised his rifle in the air and left the lodge to begin preparations for the upcoming battle.

There was no way of knowing when the attack would come. Many years ago the people had been attacked by night and were caught unaware. They had prevailed this night and fought off the attackers, but the cost was devastating. The attack had been such a surprise that entire families had been burned alive. Vengeance was slow in coming for the Shoshone and even Zacaria had participated in this hunt. The people had vowed to never be caught unaware like this again and from that time on scouts were placed here and there on high ground day and night to warn of impending danger. Actually because of the warlike nature of many of the tribes of Native Americans this was rather a common practice. The scouts would move from time to time so as not to allow an enemy the advantage of knowing their location. Over the years many lives had been spared by using this simple but effective system of warning. A sound or signal would be heard or seen from one scout to another and within minutes the entire camp would be in preparation for defense.

Angry Wolf had doubled his scouts and moved them out to double the distance. Any would be attacker would be spotted far in advance of their arrival to the camp.

Twenty eight

Zac and Pete had seen Tully step naked out of the saloon and knew Marshal Cunningham had started things moving. Bad trouble would be the order of the day for some time to come and now was as good a time as any for the two of them to do what they did best.

Spitting a stream of tobacco juice into the gutter he turned to Pete. "Reckon it's time for us to move son. Had about enough of this town anyway. We better let Cunningham and Elk know what we're about before we leave".

Pete cradled the big fifty caliber in the crook of his left arm and started down the street toward the livery. "We been killing bad folks for so long I don't even feel nothin anymore. It's like shootin' a rock or stump, you just do it. Damn shame a man has to do that. I'll get the animals ready and you do the talkin'".

Zac nodded and watched his young friend walk away. Pete was right though. After his family had been murdered the hunt for the killers had gone on far too long. It had changed them both in a way that made even their friends nervous to be around them. There had been times when they had both been covered with the blood of those they had killed while seeking vengeance for their loved ones, but there had been no other way. Perhaps one day they could stop all the killing and be clean again.

Pushing through the swinging doors of the saloon he sat down at the table with the two Marshals and poured himself a drink from the half empty bottle.

"Marshal, looks like you got things movin' a few minutes ago. We saw Tully step out into the street naked. That means war, so me and Pete are moving out now to keep an eye on things".

Cunningham had known Zac long enough to know that he and Pete did things their own way and nothing he could say would change that. He nodded and reached for the old man's hand. Zac left and the Marshal sat staring at the door as if expecting the old man to return. "Elk, you got any idea what it would be like to have those two after you? In all the years I have been at this work I have never seen any two men that dangerous". Hell, either one of them scare me".

"I never knew him before that tragedy with Pete's family but mother says he was a gentle soul. Used to be a scout for the Army. Been living with my people for a very long time. Took the place of Pete's father and taught him all he knows. Pete told me there were times during the *Long Hunt* that the two of them would be so bloody they would lay down in a stream clothes and all just to get some of the blood off. Said there were times they would ride for days caked in blood just to stay angry".

Cunningham poured himself another shoot of whisky and shook his head. "Seems to be something wrong with all that killing, but then they was cleaning up a murder and I guess it was justified. Just the same it would turn a man".

When Zac stepped out of the tavern Pet was waiting with the animals. They were out of town before either spoke. "What's the plan Zac"?

"Hell, I don't know son. Same as usual I guess. Find a spot between the people and the gang and go to work. This is a bad bunch Pete and I ain't got no intention of lettin' these bastards hurt the folks at the camp. Indians has had a bad time for years and I aim to stop part of it right now".

Pete nodded. "Yeah, well you know the country, you call it and we'll get down to business. We've been at this a good while. Think it will ever stop and just maybe we can settle down again. I would sort of like to go on back and clean our place up. Maybe start farmin' again. I miss Fawn and the baby, would like to do the graves up right and be close to them again".

Pete looked over at his old friend and saw the tears cutting a path through the dust on his face. The old man looked straight ahead and said nothing, but it was plain he wanted the same thing. "Then it's settled? When this is over we are going back".

Finally, Zac spoke. "You betcha we are". Zac spurred his pony into a gallop. "Hell son. Let's ride, we got a job to do".

Their task was going to be a grim one, but nevertheless Pete smiled and caught up to his old friend. It was almost dusk when the two made a cold camp in the rocks overlooking the road that the gang would have to take. They had done this many time in the past couple of years and knew they had to have a back way out if they were rushed. Pete took the first watch and after checking his big fifty caliber settled sown for some rest. The moon was moving toward the horizon when a soft but familiar call drew their attention. Pete picked up the fifty and smiled. "Who do you reckon that is"?

"Should know in a minute". Zac returned the call and Angry Wolf stepped out from a boulder followed by five warriors in war paint and waved.

Despite the situation the greetings were warm and while Zac spoke of things to come Pete began making coffee knowing that if the gang were anywhere near they would have already been told by Angry Wolf.

Sitting around a small smokeless fire they began to speak of the times and memories past. The tone turned serious once again and they talked long into the morning of their plans to protect the people from what was most surly coming. He and Pete spoke of the number of men that they had seen in town and of the cannon that had arrived by train the day before they had left town. They spoke of not calling in the Army knowing that to do so would bring even more treasure hunters.

"Angry Wolf, this is something we have to handle on our

own. Going to be bad, but as I see it we got no choice if the people are to have any peace at all". The warrior nodded his understanding of the situation and grasping the old timers forearm looked dead into his eyes. "We have been friends for many years bear killer. I was told of your fighting spirit from a boy and now we will stand side by side and fight yet another enemy of the people. You will know our work by the bodies of the enemy your horses must step over on the trail". Turning he gave a slight signal to his warriors and they disappeared into the morning as silently as they had come.

Zac watched them leave then looked at Pete. "Tell you one thing Pete. I wouldn't want that bunch after me for any reason. They mean business. You see the cold look in his eyes? That was pure hate Pete".

"Yeah, well I say it's about time. Let her run, and the hell with the rest of it, these bastards want fire, then let's give em' fire".

On the ride out from camp Zac thought about how much this gentle boy from southern Indiana had changed over the years and wasn't at all sure he had done the right thing in teaching him the ways of the frontier. Oh, he needed to survive and take care of his own, but Pete had turned into something much more than a scout or a hunter. He had turned into a killer as hard a man as any Zac had ever come across. Justified, yes, but a killer none the less. Had his teachings been a mistake? He silently hoped not.

It was about noon when they cut the trail of the gang and their cannon. Zac had seen those ruts in the road many times before and there was no mistaking them. The gang seemed to be moving fast and with a purpose. Their disadvantage was that they had so much gear they pretty well had to stay on the main trail and this left them vulnerable to ambush. Heading for higher ground the two men began to make their plans as they rode.

Late afternoon shadows had begun to creep out from the rocks and canyon walls when the repeated roar of the big fifty began killing the animals pulling the cannon that Tully thought would be the difference between success and failure in his hunt for the hidden gold. With the animals down Pete and Zac switched their attention to those scrambling to escape the devastating fire coming from somewhere above. It was of no use however because Lone Wolf had several hours ago placed himself and his men behind the rocks just above where the gang was now passing. Both sides were firing steadily but only Tully and his men were being either wounded or killed. Seeing the futility of the moment Tully was quick to make a decision. Removing the white silk scarf he wore around his neck he began waving it frantically back and forth in a signal of surrender. The firing stopped and Tully stepped out into the road. Raising his hands over his head he shouted to the rocks on the other side of the canyon. "I've had enough! You can keep your gold and this God forsaken country. You people are savages. Dirty savages who deserve to live in the shit hole".

Pete had pulled the hammer back and was just now preparing to blow Tully's head off when Zac reached over and put his hand on Pete's arm. "Let it go son. They've had enough. There can't be more than five or six left at the most. There's been enough blood. Let it go".

Pete eased the hammer back down and stood up. "Get movin' Tully and don't stop till you get to town. If you and your trash ain't gone by morning' the killin' won't stop until every last one of you is dead. I will drag your sorry ass out into the hills and watch as the animals eat even your bones. Now move"!

There was not another word said. Leaving the cannon and dead animals where they lay he and the rest of his men tied the dead on their horses and slowly began heading back the way they had come. It couldn't be seen from above but the mask of hate on Tully's face couldn't be hidden. This wasn't over by a long shot. His mind was no longer on the gold but revenge. Revenge of a kind that was almost unthinkable. Revenge that would include not just taking a live but of pain and blood. The killing and torture of innocents, of women and yes even children if that was what was necessary. Before this was over they would lay the gold at his feet in fear for their very families.

Twenty nine

Cunningham and Elk watched as the two headed out of town. "Deputy, we better get started after them. I have a feeling this is going to be a very bad day for Tully and his bunch. The thing is they haven't broken any law I can tell. Puts me in a bad spot as a marshal. We may need to step in and stop it if things get out of hand".

"Jack, things are already out of hand. You knew damn well what was going to happen when you started in on Tully this morning. Folks are going to die today".

"Yeah, well let's hope the ones dyin' are theirs and not ours. Spect we better move".

Hearing the fire the two put their horses into a gallop but slowed when it stopped. Heading carefully into the canyon they met Tully and four men riding out leading another four horses carrying their dead comrades. The two marshals moved aside letting them pass. When Tully came even with Cunningham he pulled up and looked first at Elk and then at Cunningham. Then, without saying a word rode on.

"You see his face Jack? This ain't over. There's more to come and it is going to be on his ground and with his rules. We need to kill him now and end this".

Cunningham nodded. "I haven't seen that kind of hate in a long time. Can't kill him though. He's been a pain in the ass, but ain't broke no laws yet. Least ways none that we can prove. We know what we know, but that ain't enough. Got to let him go".

Tully and what was left of his gang left town quickly the following morning leaving much of their gear behind. After going through it the two marshals waited for Zac and Pete to ride in and report what had happened. When they didn't show the marshals became worried and rode out to the village to check on things. It seems they had come in late and left early with two pack animals and all their belongings.

"Where you reckon they went R.E"?

"Hard to say. They've spilled a lot of blood in the last few years. Hard to get that off your hands. May be that they're headed out to start that now. Wouldn't surprise me".

Cunningham had been partially right. Zac and Pete had spent the last few years leaving a blood trail half was across the country. Right now they were riding slowly toward a darkening sky. The blood on their souls had taken its toll on both of them and both knew if it didn't end soon they would be consumed by the hate that had come to their hearts after the death of Fawn and the baby.

"I've had enough Pete. I can't do this no more. No more killin' son. We need to wash off the blood and live in peace".

Pete slowed to a stop and sat looking at the old man. "Zac, we been together a long time. Hell, you're more of a father to me than my own, but I ain't goin to let this son of a bitch hurt any of the people. I aim to kill him and be done with this. I do understand though, you ride on back to camp and I'll go this last part alone. When it's over I'll come on back and we can decide what to do then. For now, I'm ridin' on". Pete touched the brim of his hat and started out.

Zac sat for a minute and watched the young man he had ridden with for so long fade into the darkness. He smiled and started out after him knowing that anything that had to be done they would do together as always. He caught up to Pete and without looking at him muttered. "Stubborn ain't you? You sure as hell don't get that from me. Must be your mother".

The two rode for another hour and made camp for the night. The meal this night was cold and Zac sat quiet knowing that his young friend's mood was dark and sinister. The years of "*the hunt*" had changed them both and taken their toll. The old man couldn't help but wonder how much different things might have been if they had just buried Fawn and the baby and continued to build the farm. Pete's mood had grown black and mean during those years and Zac doubted he would ever again see the good natured young man that had married his daughter six years before, but the fat was in the fire now and he knew they would see it through to the end.

"We're soaked in blood Zac, I want to move on. How near over do you think this thing is"?

The question took the old man off guard and he just sat looking at Pete with his mouth open.

"There's cattle in Texas and gold in California. That bustard and his gang are scared and headed back to where they came from and those that want to stay and fight will run into the marshal and Elk". You know them two better than me, but I think the both of them will follow the gang wherever they head and end this so the people won't be bothered any more. Least that's what we would do. I've had enough, I need to wash off the blood and try to find some kind of peace".

Zac nodded. "Me too. Let's ride on back and check with R.E. and the marshal to see if things have turned around any and tell them of our plans. If things have changed we can head out. I'm ready. God knows we ain't had much time to live normal for some time. Wouldn't mind spendin' a bit of time diggin' for the yellow stuff myself. Besides the winters out there are warm and my bones ain't as limber as they used to be. When you want to head back"?

"Now".

Zac grabbed his saddle and headed for the horses. "Now it is son. Let's move before we change our minds". At that moment the awesome weight of the past years began to lift. The hate and revenge of those who had so brutally raped and murdered Pete's beautiful wife and child would eventually fade into the farthest recesses of their minds, but as with all who love unconditionally, the face and most especially the smile and sound of voice would remain forever to recall at will. Good memories do last forever.

Thirty

It took two days for the old man and Pete to reach town. Marshal Cunningham and Elk had watched from the porch of the hotel as they rode in and stepped into the street to meet them. "You two look like you been through a sticker bush. Come on in and we'll talk a spell". Cunningham poured whisky all around and leaned back in his chair looking at the two. "Well, that trash from Chicago is on the run, at least for now. Me and R.E. are planning to follow them back and end this thing once and for all. You boys have been through hell the last couple of years. What's your plan"?

Pete leaned the big fifty up against the edge of the table and rested his forearms on the table. "I can't speak for Zac, but I'm headin' out as soon as I can get a rig together. I have a lot to put behind me and I reckon to do that I need to be somewhere else".

The marshal nodded and looked at Zac. "How about you Zacaria, you going to partner with Pete or head on back to the people"?

"I love em', but everything I had there is gone now. I just about raised Pete hare and there was a time when he couldn't get along without my help. Now I can't get along without his so I reckon I'll hang with him if he'll have me. There will be a time not too far off when he will have to bury me along the tail somewhere and that is as it should be. We been through too much for me to pull out now. Hell, we might just start another ranch somewhere. Matter of fact I might just know the place".

Nothing else was said and after shaking hands the two turned and walked out into the street.

At daybreak the following day Elk and Cunningham watched as the two headed southwest out of town. "Think we'll ever see them again R.E"?

"Ain't sure, but they have earned a rest. Never seen any pair as rugged as them. Made me nervous to just be around em'. Friends or not that's a lethal pair".

Cunningham nodded. "Yeah, spect' that's about right we better get our butts in gear and head east on tomorrows train. My business with Tully ain't over. You comin or staying with your mother"?

Elk laughed. "I reckon mother is about where she belongs. Seems like them two are busy making' up for lost time. The last time I saw her and pop they were acting like a couple of newlyweds. Wouldn't surprise me if she stays on".

Darkness found the marshals making their way toward Cheyenne. It would take a full day's ride to get to the train. Cunningham had intentionally waited for Tully and what was left of his gang to be well on their way before following. Once there, it would be still another day or two before he and Elk could board the train for Indiana. This ride took five days and upon reaching the station in Crawfordsville they checked in with Bill Allison picked up a couple of horses and headed out of town for Lafayette. "R.E., you want to swing by your mothers place on West Market and check on things".

"No point in it. The neighbors will watch over things until she can get back and take care of business. Besides, Bill will keep a check on things. If there are any problems he will wire you right off".

It was after midnight before they tied up in front of the marshal's office in Lafayette. "You head on over to the hotel and turn in R.E. I'm going to check in with Tom and then I'll be on over. We can put our heads together in the morning and begin figuring this thing out". The deputy nodded and walked away. An uneasy feeling came over the marshal as he watched his young friend walk toward the hotel just across the street. It had been a long ride from Crawfordsville and Elk had been unusually quiet. Jack had been with his friend in action many times over the past few years in some tough situations and knew his serious side, but this was different, this was personal.

Tully and what was left of his gang hadn't returned directly to Chicago, but instead had left the train in Indianapolis. He knew that those he answered to wouldn't be happy that he had failed in his mission to steal the gold they had sent him after. To fail in his line of work meant only one thing and he wasn't yet ready for the consequences he knew would befall him if he continued on to Chicago. There was only one course of action for him now and that was to gather more men and go back and complete the job. He had contacts here in Indianapolis and here he would begin to rebuild his gang. He knew that the law now thought he had retreated to where he would be safe and in his element and that would now work in his favor. Never had he failed to complete a job he had been given and this would be no different. Checking into a hotel just off Washington Street he summoned first a tailor and then his men and began to formulate a plan to complete what he had been sent to do.

Thirty one

Marshal Cunningham was up early and after bathing went down to breakfast. Ha waited for Elk to join him and when he didn't, ordered his meal. It took a while to work through the steak and eggs and from time to time he looked toward the stairs expecting to see Elk coming to join him. When he didn't show the marshal became a bit agitated and pushing his plate back got up and headed upstairs. There was no response from the knocking on Elks door so he turned the knob and walked in only to find the young man gone. Swearing, he flew down stairs and headed for the livery. "My deputy been in here this mornin'Jeb".

"Yep, came in a little after three this mornin', rolled me out of bed , paid me, saddled up and rode out without sayin' more than a couple of words. Had a grim look about him though and I did notice he headed south. That tell you anything Marshal"?

"Saddle my horse, will you Jeb? I'll be back shortly". No more than twenty minutes passed before he was back and ready to ride out. "Which way was he headed Jeb"? A useless question though, he already knew the answer. Heeling the horse he headed southeast at a gallop. He figured Elk couldn't be any farther than Monroe or maybe Colfax, but still he a sizeable head start. He also knew the fences here in the Midwest would not allow him to cut across country so he slowed his pace and continued on to where he knew Elk would be. Thinking about the murder of Oliver and the abuse to his mother Jack knew this was personal to his young friend and that before this was over there would be plenty of blood spilled. The thing that concerned him most was that these gangsters were not only brutal, but smart as well. This wouldn't be anything like tracking a couple of rustlers or bank robbers. These men would stand and fight because that was what they were paid to do, and besides they were on their home ground, a different situation all together. Unknowingly he picked up the pace once again.

Just passing through Thorntown, the young marshal stopped to give his mount a breather and make some coffee. Thinking about the situation that faced him, he became grim and angry. Oliver was murdered before his eyes and his mother though now safe had been brutally kidnapped and beaten. He was not sure what he would find in Indianapolis, but figured Rena might give him an idea where to start. Starting out once more he rode to Whitestown and decided to stop for the night before cutting south to Brownsburg. Building a small fire and making coffee he leaned back against his saddle and began thinking about what was ahead and how to handle it. Once again the thought of Rena and sleep found him with a smile on his face still thinking of her.

Jack Cunningham came across his deputy's fire about two hours before daylight. Rode up, and sat looking down at Elk who at this minute was sipping coffee and eating a slightly burned biscuit. "You gonna get down and have some coffee or just sit there looking at me? By the way, you look like crap".

"Damn you R.E., what in the hell do you think you're doing? You think you can take this gang on all by yourself? Tully is in Chicago by now and here you are headin' in the wrong direction, or you just out seein' the country? You work for me deputy, and you do nothing unless I tell you to do it. You might just get this badge of mine someday, but for now you work for me, and don't you forget it".

Elk looked first at the fire then back at the marshal and stood up. "I don't much like your tone Jack. My dad was murdered and mother was kidnapped by these bastards and I aim to settle the score anyway I have to. As for your damn badge you can have it. Stick it where it will do the most good as far as I'm concerned. Now, stop all this bullshit and get down and have some breakfast, we need to talk. Besides you've tuckered that horse plum out. Don't look to me like he could go another mile"

Cunningham watched as the unsaddled horse rolled a few times and began to graze. Poured a cup of coffee and grabbed a biscuit. "These ain't near as good as Nancy's, you should've stayed home long enough to learn to cook. Now, tell me what it is you're doing here anyway. And I ain't going any farther until I get a couple of hours sleep. So make it fast"

Elk smiled and slapping his friend on the back sat back down. "Here's how I see it. Tully and his bosses are in Chicago. Where, we don't know, but what we do know is that they have contacts in Indianapolis. I figure if we can get to them and have a talk they will be able to point us in the right direction. Rena might just be able to give us a name or two and that is where we could start".

Elk looked over at jack and the marshal's smile stopped him short. "What's so funny"?

This time Cunningham laughed out loud. "You ain't kiddin' me none pard. You're heading to Indianapolis cause you want to see Rena again. You're horny, ain't that right"?

Elk's eyes narrowed and his tone took on a serious note". "You mean to tell me you think that's why I rode all this way? To have sex with Rena"?

"Damn straight".

"My god Jack, you ain't changed a bit. All you ever think about is that damn trombone of yours, whisky, and sex. There are more important things you know. Like the job at hand".

"May be, but that ain't what's on your mind right now. Admit it you're horny for Rena".

"I ain't admitting nothing you old fool. Get some sleep we

got a lot of planning to do and a ways to ride yet. And ain't horny for Rena".

"Of course not deputy".

Thirty two

Tully was once again in his element, fancy hotel room, tailored suits and the best of food. He had sent men throughout the city rounding up those ready to do his dirty work. He knew the two marshals would return home after he had left Wyoming. He wasn't sure about Cunningham, but he was sure the half breed would follow. The killing of his father and kidnapping of his mother had been so badly handled it had become a personal matter with the young man. Tully also believed the young man would follow him seeking his revenge and he decided it would be better to handle it here than in Chicago. After all, here he had to answer to know one, so this is where it would end. All he had to do now was alert his gang and wait.

It was sometime after daybreak the two saddled up and headed for Brownsburg and Indianapolis. Cunningham rode quiet for a time then asked. "Where we headed R.E., I mean if you ain't horny like you said we will need to check into a hotel. If that's the case we need to take these badges off and pick out a couple of names so folks won't suspect nothing"?

"You know damn well where we're headed Jack, and you can knock that crap off right now".

"Uh huh, just asking, no need to get worked up. After all, you're the one that got all red in the face after your first visit. Your mother picked up on that right away".

"Jack".

"Okay, okay. This is your fight R.E. I ain't got any real steak in this. Tully hasn't officially broken any law and I can't arrest him on anything. I can shoot him, but I can't arrest him".

"I figure we will wait till nightfall to go in. be safer for Rena and give us a chance to look around a bit. If we can find one of Tully's men we might get something we can use before we head north".

Reaching the White River they once again made coffee and waited for darkness. Around eight o'clock they headed for Rena's place just off of Indiana Avenue. When they arrived there was a party of some kind so they used the entrance that Rena's butler Mr. Franklin had shown him. Walking through a short hallway they entered a door that led directly into the butler's pantry and waited. In just a short time Mr. Franklin came in with some empty trays. Elk stepped from behind the door and gently took hold of the old man's arm. "Mr. Franklin, it's me, Richard Running Elk". The old man didn't even flinch, but turned with a smile and put his finger to his lips for them to be quiet then motioned for them to follow him. He opened a small door in the pantry exposing some very steep stairs and again motioned for them to follow.

Cunningham was impressed. "Damn R.E. these folks are sneaky".

Mr. Franklin once again motioned for them to be quiet and continued on up the stairs. Arriving at the top he whispered for them to wait and quickly walked a few steps to a room off the balcony. Opening the door they hunkered down and duck walked the twenty steps or so and entered the room. Once inside he shook hands with Elk and turned to Cunningham. "And who might you be sir"?

Shaking hands with the old man Jack introduced himself as U.S. Marshal Jack Cunningham from Lafayette.

"I see, well Mr. Cunningham I expect you gentlemen could use a bite to eat and a bath. There is a tub in that room there with hot running water. I will return shortly".

After eating, both men bathed, put on clean clothes and sat waiting for Rena to appear. When she did the look between her and Elk was obvious and Cunningham smiled. Elk gave him a glare and his face straightened a bit,

"Rena, this is marshal Cunningham, we've been partners

for some time".

Walking over she took Jacks hand. "Welcome to my home Marshal, what I can do to help you and Richard, please, sit down and tell me how I can help. Did you know that Richards's mother saved my family from slavery several years ago? A very brave woman Nancy Weliever, I was sorry to hear of her trouble and pray she is well".

"She is well, moved a bit further west though. Actually, she's the reason we're here. You see the gang that kidnapped her and murdered Elks father are located in Chicago, we don't have any idea where and thought we might ask a few questions of those that work for them here to try and get some idea of their whereabouts".

"I see, and how can I help in that regard"?

"R.E. here tells me that you know most of the influential folks living in Indianapolis and we thought you might have an idea who to talk to about this".

Rena smiled and jack could see why his young was in love with her. Her grace and beauty was something to behold and it was plain that she was intelligent to boot. Jack looked over at his deputy and this time it was he who was smiling. Clearing his throat he continued. "We don't mean to put you out any Rena, but any information you can give us will be of help".

"It's a bit late to start now, but we can continue in the morning. I will have Franklin open a room for Richard and if this room suits you, you can stay here. Franklin will wake you for breakfast and we will begin again". When the door closed behind her jack turned to look at R.E.

"Richard, I have never seen a woman as beautiful as her in my life. No wonder you wanted to come here".

"Stop calling me Richard and that's not why I came here".

"Whatever you say Richard. I for one am turnin' in".

Jack was up early and was sipping coffee when Elk walked into the dining room and sat down across from him. Elk had a sheepish look on his face and Cunningham couldn't resist. My god, R.E., you're disgusting you know that"?

"Go to hell Jack".

"I might at that deputy".

"Good morning gentlemen, I apologize for being late, but I always bathe before breakfast. Franklin, I hope you have something special for us this morning, I for one am starved".

Again, Jack couldn't resist. "How about you Richard, are you starved as well"?

The deputy tried to play it off, but it didn't work. He did manage to give his boss what he considered to be a warning stare. Rena glanced at the two and took the moment in stride.

"Marshal, we are all adults here don't you think"?

"I do Rena, it's just that in all the years I have known R.E. here, I have never seen him act like this before. I think the closest he has ever been to anything as beautiful as you may have been a wild mare in the mountains of Wyoming".

"I see. Well, to tell you the truth I can't ever remember being compared to a horse, but I will nevertheless take that as a complement. Now, perhaps we should get started on the problem at hand and see if we can find where this Tully character might be staying in Chicago".

Franklin had finished setting their plates in front of them then walked over and stood behind Rena's chair. "If you will excuse me ma'am, if you are referring to the gangster from Chicago perhaps I can be of some service. He is not in Chicago, but staying right here in Indianapolis. If my information is correct, he is presently a guest in a hotel somewhere in the city. I don't recall the hotel but I did get the impression it was somewhere close to Union Station. There are several hotels in the area. It seems that he and his friends arrived a few days ago".

Jack looked at Elk and then at Franklin. "Just how do you

know this Mr. Franklin"?

Well sir, we do get a lot of society folks in here and not all of them are what we would call upstanding citizens, but then we can't pick and choose who comes and goes as we are a social gathering place in the city. At the party last evening I overheard one of our not so upstanding guests bragging to another gentleman that he had been approached by one of Mr. Tully's representatives offering a rather large sum of money to accompany him on a journey somewhere in the west. It hadn't occurred to me until now that this information might be of interest to you gentlemen".

Elk jumped to his feet so violently his chair flew back against the wall". Franklin, would you fetch my gunbelt. I have business in the city".

"And just what the hell are you going do marching up and down Main Street with your gun strapped on asking about Tully where there could be a dozen hired guns who know you on sight. Sit your young ass back down in that chair and let's talk this thing out".

Elk knew he was right. He would most probably be killed before he could get a half a block. Picking up his chair he returned to the table and sat down.

Rena had been quiet through all of this but she knew the marshal was right and said so. "Richard, the marshal is right. This city surly isn't the wild west, but we aren't exactly as refined as we might be either, as a matter of fact the criminal element here has quite a bit of influence in local politics and the death of a stranger in this city wouldn't cause more than raised eyebrows for a day or two. It would be forgotten and you would be buried in an unmarked grave if someone hadn't claimed you in the first two hours".

Franklin returned and handed Elk his gun belt. Pulling the colt from the holster he checked it, spun the cylinder then placed it on the table and sat down. "So, what's the plan?

Sooner or later Tully is going to start back after the gold and I'm not going to let him get within five hundred miles of my father and mother. I'm telling you now Jack, if I see the bastard on the street I'll kill him and to hell with the consequences".

"R.E., we're the law here and we have certain responsibilities to the people of this town. To the state for that matter, so I don't want to hear any more of that kind of talk or I'll take that badge off you and finish this thing myself. You know as well as I do that Tully hasn't broken any laws yet and until he does you are going to stay away from him. We'll get him and the rest of them, but it has to be done legally. There are a lot of innocent people who get in the way of that kind of thinking and most of the time they are the ones who end up getting hurt. Agreed"?

"You're the boss Jack, but if it goes sour, I'm going to do it my way".

Jack looked at Rena and shook his head. "You ever see anyone that stubborn Rena"?

"Only one person and that was years ago. Drove a wagon all the way to Minnesota carrying a shotgun pulled by the biggest mules and sided by the biggest dog I have ever seen. As I recall her name was Nancy".

Cunningham laughed. "Well pard, at least you come by it honest. Come to think about it you do sound like your mother when you get wound up. Now, let's get down to business, we got some marshalin' to do".

Thirty three

Tully and what was left of his gang had checked into one of Indianapolis's finest hotels located just off Washington Street and his first act was to call a local tailor to get himself outfitted, he then sent his men throughout the city rounding up for replacements for those lost in the canyons of Wyoming. That done he ordered food and settled down to figure out his next move. He knew contacting his bosses in Chicago wasn't an option at this point, because they wouldn't understand. This wasn't a matter of settling a score with a rival gang or putting the squeeze on a rich business man, this was dealing with people as dangerous as anyone he had ever come across. These people didn't hesitate to shoot first from ambush and gave no quarter. A tactic that he himself had used to his advantage. Ruthlessness used in the city promoted fear and quick results, but this was useless in the west, these people responded with equal force and besides this was their ground. Lighting a cigar he leaned back in the overstuffed chair and pondered his next move. The prize was gold and his bosses had sent him after it. To fail would most surly cost him his life, besides, he had spent his adult life building his reputation and wasn't about to tuck his tail and run. Not for these hicks, not for anyone.

Jack and Elk decided to make no contact with the local constabulary because some of those who were supposed to be enforcing the law might be on the payroll of those they were supposed to be investigating. The taverns north and south of Washington, New York, and West streets were numerous it would have been much quicker to split up and check them, but the two decided to work together for safety. Starting on Washington Street they hit pay dirt in the second tavern. Cunningham took the back door and after waiting for him to get in place Elk walked through the front door. No sooner had he stepped through the door a member of Tully's gang recognized him and bolted for the back. Turning, the young marshal walked back through the door and around the side of the building to the back. No sooner did he turn the corner than he spotted the man's feet sticking out past the wall. "You didn't kill him did you Jack"?

"No pard, we're just havin' a little talk is all. Came busting out this door and ran right in to the barrel of my gun with his head. I'm surprised this bunch gets anything done as stupid as they are".

"Uh huh, and how did the barrel of your Dragoon get stuck in his mouth? Looks like you're scaring him a bit. He might have been with that bunch in the canyon. Better take it out of his mouth, he's already pissed his pants".

Jack holstered his gun and jerking the man to his feet threw him against the wall. Stepping forward he placed his hand to hold him up. "Where's your boss ass hole"?

Jacks pistol had knocked out one of the man's upper teeth and split his lips. Blood ran down his chin and onto the front of his shirt. Still, he was defiant. "Go to hell hillbilly, I ain't tellin' you nothin'.

Elk drew his bone handled knife and stepping forward cut the man's belt letting his pants fall to his ankles. Both men looked and then laughed. "Damn pard, you ain't got no underwear, and from the looks of it you ain't got much of anything else either. Tell you what, you tell us where your boss is and we don't ruin your little manhood there".

"Like I said halfbreed, I ain't tellin' you nothin. You might as well let me go and clear out. Go on back to them slut squaws where you came from".

"Wrong answer, you piece of shit"!

Hearing Elk speak through his teeth Jack reached out just in time and stopped him from slitting the man's throat. "Mr. this halfbreed as you call him is just about to slit your

throat. Now me on the other hand, well, I'm a bit more civilized than that. Deputy, will you please hand me your knife"? Knife in hand Jack ran the back edge of the blade down the man's cheek and on further down ending up by resting the point on the man's privates. "You doubt about what I am about to do to you mister? You see, I'm the law here and I can do anything I want. If I cut your wanger off it will be all legal like. Now, where is your boss staying"? This time the man was quiet. Covered with sweat he couldn't wait to tell what he knew. "He's not my boss, I work for someone else but I hear he's stayin' in some fancy hotel off of Washington Street somewhere".
"Which one exactly"?
"I don't know, honest. He made the rest of us move into some fleabag a couple of blocks away. He don't spend much time with us unless he wants to give us orders".
"But you can find him if you heed too, right"?
"No, but my boss knows where is. Please marshal don't kill me, I have a wife and kids".
"You should have thought of that before you hooked up with this bunch. You ain't got much of a future in this business bud, might want to find another line of work. We're not going to kill you, but we are going to use you to send a message to Tully. Jack spent the next few seconds cutting the man's clothes off him leaving him standing naked except for his shoes and socks. "Okay bud, you go and tell your boss that we are in town and are coming after Tully. One more thing, if we see you anywhere in town we will just shoot you on sight and be done with it. Now start moving".
The man stood in front of them buck naked trying to cover himself as best he could. "Marshal, you ain't really going to do this are you? I mean, it just ain't right for Pete sake, there's people all over the street up there"! Squaring his shoulders and crossing his arms on his chest he stood there

looking at them both. "I ain't doing it".

Pulling his Dragoon from the holster Jack pointed it at the man's privates and pulled back the hammer. "You sure about that bud"?

Watching the man running naked up the main street of Indianapolis brought a chuckle from both men. Turning back toward Rena's jack was quiet for a while. "Couldn't let you kill him R, E, we needed the information".

Elk slapped his friend on the back and laughed. "I ain't never letting you use my knife again. You embarrass folks with your crude ways. You should be ashamed of yourself. His boss will most likely kill him anyway for what he told us".

"Might be, nut at least we didn't do it. He was just a messenger anyway. Harmless guy trying to make a living. I hate it when folks like that get used. You see the calluses on his hands, most likely works a small piece of ground somewhere. I wish him luck".

"You goin soft in your old age Jack"?

"No, but times are hard and some folks do things they don't want to do just to get by".

"Just wondering".

"Go to hell smart ass".

When they reached Rena's, Franklin opened the door. "Good evening gentlemen. I trust your search was fruitful"?

Jack stopped and turned to the butler. "Mr. Franklin, do you always talk that fancy"?

"Well sir, I have worked for some very fancy people and I guess one just naturally takes on the ways of those one is around".

Before he could answer Elk spoke up. "Franklin, Jack's getting soft. I guess it's because he's getting old".

"Aaaaahh"! And the marshal stomped up the stairs toward his room. "Sleep light tonight deputy, anything might

happen. Besides, you need to watch out for this old man".
Elk looked at Franklin. "That's true. I do, I really do. A shame too, but sooner or later I guess age gets us all".
"Of course sir, will there be anything else sir"?
"I guess that it. Oh, has Rena already turned in"?
"Yes sir, some time ago. Said she would see you in the morning".
The look on Franklins face told the young deputy all he needed to know.
"Well then, good night Mr. Franklin". "Good night sir".

Thirty four

Tully had finished the business of the day and gave orders that he wasn't to be disturbed for the rest of the evening. Alone, he was just getting started on his meal when the knock on the door came. Grumbling, he walked over and jerked it open. "This better damn well be important". There stood two of his men and between them was the naked man Jack and Elk had talked to earlier. Stepping back he ordered the men into the room. His mind flashed back to his own episode in the saloon sometime earlier; knowing the answer before he asked it. "Just what the hell is this"? One of the two started to speak but Tully cut him off with a wave of his hand. "Big man with a big pistol and an Indian, right".

"Yes sir".

"What did they want"?

"Wanted to know where you were. Couldn't tell them cause I didn't know".

"And that, my naked friend is what has just saved your life". Tully pulled some money out of his pocket handing it to the man. Go downstairs and tell the clerk I said to go and get you some clothes. Turning his back on the man he went back to his dinner, took a bite and threw his napkin on the plate. "This is cold, order me another".

"What happens now boss"?

Tully smiled and looked over at the two. "We kill them, I know right where they are. Now, get my dinner".

It was after two in the morning when a strong hand clamped over Cunningham's mouth. Franklin whispered. "Marshal, there's men in the house. I'm going to be outside of Miss Rena's room. I'll leave the rest to you". Franklin turned to leave and Jack could see the outline of a shotgun clutched in his right hand. Rolling out of bed he knew there would be no time to lose, but he couldn't hurry either for fear of tipping off whoever had broken in. The dragoon clutched in his fist he opened the bedroom door and slipped out into the hall heading for Elks room, but stopped when he saw the two men crouched by the banister at the head of the stairs. They hadn't seen him yet, but they had spotted Franklin at the end of the hall standing just outside of Rena's room. Both barrels of Franklin's shotgun went off with a deafening boom hitting the two men so hard they were thrown through the rail to the floor below. Jack looked down ready to fire, but could see they were cut to pieces. Elk joined him and they could hear Franklin telling Rena to stay in her room for now. She pushed his arm aside and walked to the rail as well.

"Is this Tully's work"?

It seems Jack had put his hat on before leaving his room and was now standing in his red long johns holding the big dragoon. Elk was standing next to Rena looking at him. "Damn, Jack, you always sleep dressed like that? With all that red underwear, and your hat and gun. No wonder you don't have any social life. That would scare a woman half to death. You have got to do something about that. I bet Franklin could help you with that. How about it Mr. Franklin, you'd help the Marshal with his wardrobe wouldn't you"?

"Be happy to sir. We'll start the first thing in the morning".

"This ain't funny deputy. Get dressed, we got work to do, and Franklin do you think we might have some coffee while we figure this thing out? By the way, what kind of load did you have in that shotgun anyway"?

"I'm not exactly sure sir, the gunsmith over on Alabama street does the loads. All he ever tells me is that the loads will do their job".

Jack looked back over the rail and shook his head. "Yeah, well he was right about that. Elk, we better send for the local law and get this mess cleaned up. Don't look like there will be much to it seeing as how these two broke in here in the middle of the night".

"I'll get the law, but you still need better underwear, and we still don't know where Tully is, but he sure as hell knows where we are".

It took less than an hour for the local police to make their assessment and load the bodies into a wagon headed for the undertakers place. They were ready to leave when Jack approached the officer in charge. "Anyway of telling who these two were"?

"I know who they were marshal, local trash who hire out for any amount of money. Belong to a local bunch that has big dreams of running things here. Extortion, murder, prostitution, that sort of thing. You did the city a favor tonight. Be on your guard though, they won't take lightly to your killing two of their own. By the way, what tore them up that way"?

"Special load".

"I see, well keep it handy".

By five they were still at the table working out a plan. "Jack, here's how I see it. We don't know where Tully is, we have killed two of the local gang members, meaning we now have more than one fight, and Rena's now in danger for letting us stay here. Rena is either going to need protection or she is going to have to stay somewhere until this thing is over".

Franklin had been standing quietly to one side of Rena's chair. "Excuse me gentlemen, but Miss Rena will need to do neither. Over the years we have had our share of trouble and have through necessity made provisions to take care of our own. If you will allow me I will make the necessary provisions to handle the care of Miss Rena".

Rena smiled and patted the old man's hand. "In a half an hour Franklin will have a small army of our friends here. It would be foolish of anyone to try and harm either me or this property, and that includes your Mr. Tully".

She was right, in less than thirty minutes every porch chair, lawn chair, and kitchen chair held someone with a shotgun or rifle handy.

Satisfied that she was safe, Elk and Jack waited until after daylight, then mounted up and rode about five miles out of town making camp off the beaten path where they could make some kind of a plan.

"Pard, you know this son of a bitch has us over a barrel don't you. We can't make a move without him knowing about it. Makes us sittin' ducks".

Elk grinned at him. "Uh huh, and that's why you waited till daylight to ride all the way out here in the country to camp. You don't plan to catch one of these folks trying to kill us and ask a few questions, or are we really camping just for the fun of it"?

"I figure Tully will know of our whereabouts shortly, if he doesn't know already. Knowin' him he will wait till dark and then hit us. Our problem is we don't know how many there will be. We could well be killed right here R.E".

"Yeah, well it's as good a place to die as any I reckon. We been in tough spots before Jack, you know that".

"We're out in the open here pard, but anyone comin' at us will be in the open too, so we just have to kill as many as we can and bring this thing to a close. I'm tired of playin' games with this bastard. If they come at night we'll catch em' in a cross fire. If in the daylight we'll set up behind those downed limbs over there and pick em' off one by one. Ain't much of a plan, but I need to get this over with".

Tully's men had hired eight additional guns and on Tully's order had brought them to his hotel room for orders. In thirty minutes fourteen men were heading out of town on the road that the two marshals had taken a few hours before, intending to ride until they had overtaken and killed both Jack and Elk. It took less tan an hour to come across the camp. Both marshals were in plain sight and stood watching as the gang came to a stop two hundred yards away.

As Tully swung his horse around to give orders both marshals moved to the cover of the fallen tree limbs and opened fire with lever action rifles. Five of the fourteen were down within seconds and the remaining nine came out of their saddles and hit the ground running for cover. Fire began coming from all directions at once causing Jack and Elk to drop down and take what limited cover there was.

"Hot damn, we're in it now R.E., this is what these badges are all about"

Elk grinned at his friend as he shoved more cartridges into the repeater. "Your nuts Jack. You know that? It'll be dark soon and we can take the fight to them. There's no cover for them to move to now so we should be alright for the time being".

"Aim just below the rifle flash that will get a few more of them, and keep moving so they don't get a good shot. You're a smart ass, but I would hate to lose you after all this time, your mother would never forgive me".

It took about forty five minutes for darkness to set in and they could hear Tully's men begin moving about. Elk pulled his hair back and tied it with a piece of rawhide. After rubbing dirt on his face and hands he tucked his colt into his belt and pulled the bone handled knife and moved closer to Jack he whispered. "Time to go, see you directly". The look each gave the other said all there was to say. This was deadly business and each man knew it. Going on his belly Elk began to crawl off to the right. It took only seconds before he was out of sight. Pulling his dragoon, Jack would mix rifle fire with pistol fire hoping to give Elk time to get behind the gang. He could see the fire moving further and further to his left and knew it would just be a matter of time before they flanked him.

Elk hadn't gone fifty yards before he saw the first man. Jacks fire had been mostly on the left to keep Elk as safe as possible and he knew the Indian wouldn't fire and give away his position. When fire came from the right the Marshal intentionally fired over the head of the shooter. With Elk snaking through the knee high grass it was all but impossible to see him and this he used to his advantage. The man he had just come upon was squatted down so he could fire and drop to the ground. Elk crawled right up behind the man and in an instant had grabbed him and in one movement had slit the man's throat. Easing him to the ground he moved on to the next man and because of the darkness and the fact that Tullies men were in the open on this moonless night it wasn't long before the fire on the right had stopped completely.

Tully was no fool and he too had noticed the fire on the right had stopped. Having seen this Indian in action before and experienced the fury of the two frontiersmen cutting down his men in the canyons of Wyoming he instinctively knew his men were either dead or hurt so badly they couldn't fire. Cursing and giving the order to withdraw he mounted his horse and headed for town. The others followed but two of the three remaining were cut down by Elk's colt. He had gotten within ten feet of these men and when they mounted he had simply stood up and cut them down.

The Marshal walked up and put his big hand on Elk's shoulder, "Damn R.E. I sure as hell would hate to have you come after me. You have blood all over you, better get that washed off before we get back. Stopping at White river Elk waded in and washed as much of the blood off his clothing as possible. Jack ad built a small fire and walking up the bank Elk sat down warming himself. Jack looked over at his young friend and smiled. "What goes through your mind when you're doing that kind of work? I don't mind

killin' bad men, but what you is different. Is it some kind of Indian thing R.E."?
Elk sat staring into the fire for a minute before he answered. "My people didn't always have the weapons white people used. We had the knife, the spear, and the arrow and we learned how to use them in war. Blood runs and people die, that's all, nothin more".
Jack nodded his understanding and nothing more was said.

Thirty five

Dawn found the two pulling up in front of Rena's place, dismounting they walked up the steps and past those who had come to defend her. The look of the Marshal and his deputy told them all they needed to know. Greeting them at the door Franklin said a bath and breakfast would be ready after they had cleaned up a bit. "Miss Rena doesn't like dirty folks sitting at her table. Your baths will be ready shortly gentlemen".

After breakfast both men walked out onto the porch to talk in private. Elk spoke first and his voice had iron in the tone. "We need to finish this Jack and we need to finish it today".

"You got a plan pard, or do you want to just walk over to the Hotel and kill the son of a bitch"?

"The young marshal started walking and talking at the same time. "That is exactly what I want to do and I want to do it right now"?

Following the Marshal checked his dragoon and said, "Well hell, why did you say so? I could use a drink anyway".

Arriving at the hotel they found Tully had checked out about an hour before. He was neither there nor was he even in town. They learned he had taken the train to Chicago and sent whatever men he had left back to where they came from.

"Looks like we are going to Chicago Jack, you want to take the train or ride"?

"That's about two hundred miles, what say we put the horses on the next train and when this is over take a slow ride back. Nice country between here and there".

The train pulled into Chicago about two in the morning and the site of these two men dressed in western garb riding down the street was quite a sight. So much so that it didn't take long for Tully to find out the two were in town. This didn't matter however because that is exactly what they wanted. It had also been reported to local law enforcement and the remembrance of the last time Elk had been in town was mentioned. The sight of this huge lawman who carried a pistol half as long as his leg and an Indian with braided hair and a Colt strapped to his leg, and a very large knife resting between his shoulder blade was not something one would ordinarily see on these sophisticated Chicago streets. Pulling up in front of a restaurant the two tied their horses and went inside for some morning coffee and an early breakfast.

"Well we're here R.E. where are we supposed to find this Mr. Tully anyway, and what do we do with him when we do find him"?

The young Marshal didn't hesitate. "I don't know what you are going to do Jack, but I intend to kill him and anyone who stands with him".

"Just like that"?

"Just like that, he killed some of my people and has threatened my father, and his time has come to an end".

"Huhuh and where do you think we might find him".

"He will find us, wouldn't be surprised if he doesn't already know we are here and has someone watching us right now".

As it turned out Elk was right, when they left the restaurant they saw a man about half a block away standing watching them. Mounting up they rode slowly toward the man and when they were close enough both men slipped the leather off their pistol hammers just in case there was trouble.

"He is gonna run R.E, you get ready to head him off, we need the information".

The Marshal was right; as they approached the man bolted and had it not been for Elk cutting him out like a calf to be branded he would have gotten away, as it was he was hit with the front shoulder of Elks horse and fell hard to the ground. Marshal Cunningham dismounted and pulling his dragoon leaned over and sticking it into the man's mouth and in his usual good natured way said, "Howdy friend, we would like to ask you a question or two if you don't mind". Elk smiled and said, "Damn Jack you sure do know how to make friends". No wonder you are alone most of the time, between that Dragoon of yours and your trombone it's a wonder people even talk to you".

The Marshal nodded and pulling the pistol out of the man's mouth said, "Where is Tully, he sent you to watch us and you have done your job, now where is he"?

This man was an easterner and the sight of these two standing over him was more than he could handle, but he knew if he told them what they wanted to know Tully would either kill him or have his men do it. "I don't know who you're talking about, let me go or I will tell the police".

Jack stuck the Dragoon back into the man's mouth and pulled the hammer back. "I ain't gonna ask you but this last time mister, where is Tully"?

Elk stepped forward and put his hand on the Marshal's arm and said, "Wait a minute Jack if you pull the trigger on that cannon we will have the police all over us, let me talk to him".

The Marshal stepped back and reaching behind has back Elk pulled the foot long knife from between his shoulders, leaned over the man and grabbing a fistful of his hair and shaved it off at the scalp. "Mister, look at me, I am an Indian and don't give a damn about anything but finding out where your boss is right now. You don't tell us what we want to know I am going to scalp you right here, right now. Now you son of a bitch where is your boss"? The look in Elks eyes was all the man needed to see.

"If I tell you he will kill me".

Elk moved the knife to the man's throat, "Make your choice mister".

"He's in the hotel down by the river, the River Hotel on the second floor. Now let me go".

Elk put the knife back in the sheath and stepped away from the man.

Leaping to this feet the man ran and kept running until he was out of sight.

"Where you reckon he will go Jack".

"Back in the hole with the rest of the rats I suppose, we going to finish this now R.E."?

"That's what we came for, I am to finish this once and for all".

"You know he is going to have men all over that hotel don't you? How are we going to get to him without getting killed"?

"We aren't, I am, and you are going to do what you do best and that is cause a commotion to distract his men so I can get to the second floor and corner the bastard".

Mounting up the men rode the short distance to the river and pulled up about a block from the hotel, secured their mounts and walked the rest of the way.

Marshal Cunningham checked his pistol and patting his friend on the back said, "Wait to move until after you see it" and stepped off into the Shadows of a soon to be breaking dawn.

As with all hotels this one had a work shed setting behind it where materials were stored by the maintenance people and pulling the door open Jack stepped inside and lit a match. Finding turpentine, kerosene, wood, and rags for cleaning he smiled, dumped the cans over and dropped the match. In less than thirty seconds the fire was roaring and the small building was in flames. Walking to the front door of the hotel he stepped inside and yelled FIRE at the top of his lungs and then stepped back outside and returned to where he had left Elk.

Watching the maintenance shed in flames and the women screaming, and men running outside in their long underwear brought a smile to Jacks face. "That ought to do it R.E., it's all yours now pard".

Elk had watched as well from the shadows of the carriage house located to the back and side of the hotel and just as he was ready to move he saw Tully come out the back door dressed in an expensive robe and carrying a small revolver in his hand. Beside him was his body guard carrying a double barrel scatter gun. Elk waited until they were in the open then stepped out of the shadows facing them. Tully stopped short surprised to see him.

"Well if it isn't our young deputy come to visit. Last I heard you were miles from here". Tullie's hand moved ever so slightly showing his intent; Elk saw the move, but didn't bat an eye. "What brings you here now deputy"?

"I've come to put an end to this murdering business of yours Tully. I'm here to kill you". With that the body guard brought the scatter gun up but before he could pull the trigger the right side of his head exploded from the impact of the 44 slug from Jacks pistol.

Tully jerked his gun up to fire but stopped looking down at the bone handle now protruding from his chest. Looking back at Elk he opened his mouth to say something, but nothing came out and without a word he fell forward on his face.

Elk walked over and with the toe of his boot turned Tully over, removed the knife and wiping it clean on the expensive robe placed it back in the sheath resting between his shoulder blades.

Riding out of town both were quiet and it was some time before Jack spoke. "You know Tullywill just be replaced don't you"?

"Yep, but I figure there will be a lot of killin' between

themselves before they get organized again. He was the meanest son of a bitch I have ever seen".

"What you goin to do now R.E., head home"?

"After a bit I reckon thought I might see the country before I catch the train".

Jack laughed and took a swig from the bottle he always carried for medicinal purposes. "You mean your goin back to see Rena before you head home, is that it"?

"Your nosy Jack you know that"?

The ride back to Lafayette was peaceful and quiet though they did keep a watchful eye out for trouble. When they came to the Wabash River each said their goodbyes and Elk headed for Rena's place in Indianapolis.

At that moment two thousand miles to the west Nancy and the Chief stood holding hands jumping from the deafening blast of dynamite that roared through the canyons not too distant from the village they watched as the dust cleared. Gently taking her face in his hands he kissed her lips and whispered, "It is finished my love, it is finished".

This story is fiction, but make no mistake according to legend there was much gold transported by those who walked this continent for hundreds of years before it was officially discovered.

Does it remain hidden among the bones of those left behind to guard it? One might do well to remember that legends are often nothing more than memories handed down from one generation to the next.

The gold is still there!

End

This book, is the second in a series, the first being "*In search of Home*, the third *"Weliever's Railroad* which is now being written and the fourth which is now in the drafting stage will be *"The long Hunt"*.

Made in the USA
Las Vegas, NV
05 December 2022